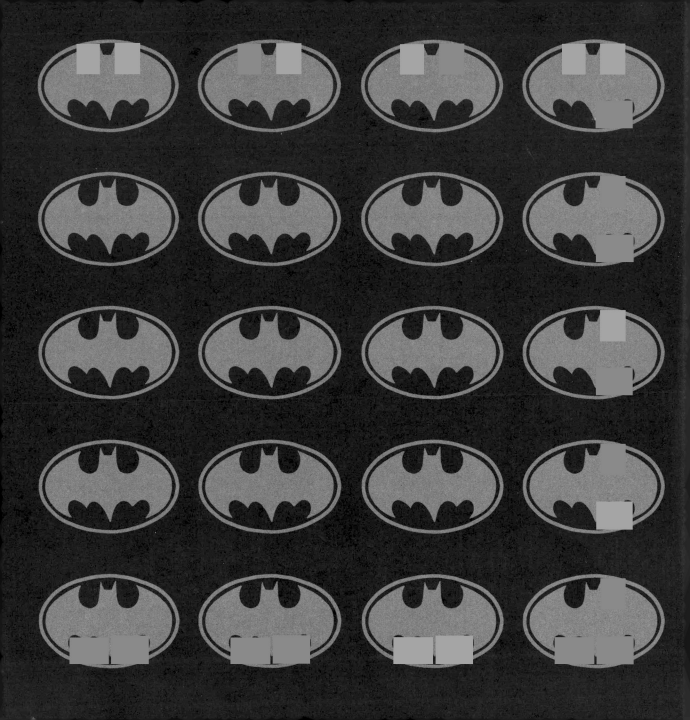

STORIES CHANGE THE WORLD

I am Batman™

BATMAN—
THE DARK KNIGHT—
WAS CREATED BY
BOB KANE WITH
BILL FINGER.
FINGER WROTE THE
FIRST BATMAN
STORY AND KANE
RENDERED THE
ARTWORK.

BRAD MELTZER
illustrated by Christopher Eliopoulos

DIAL BOOKS FOR YOUNG READERS

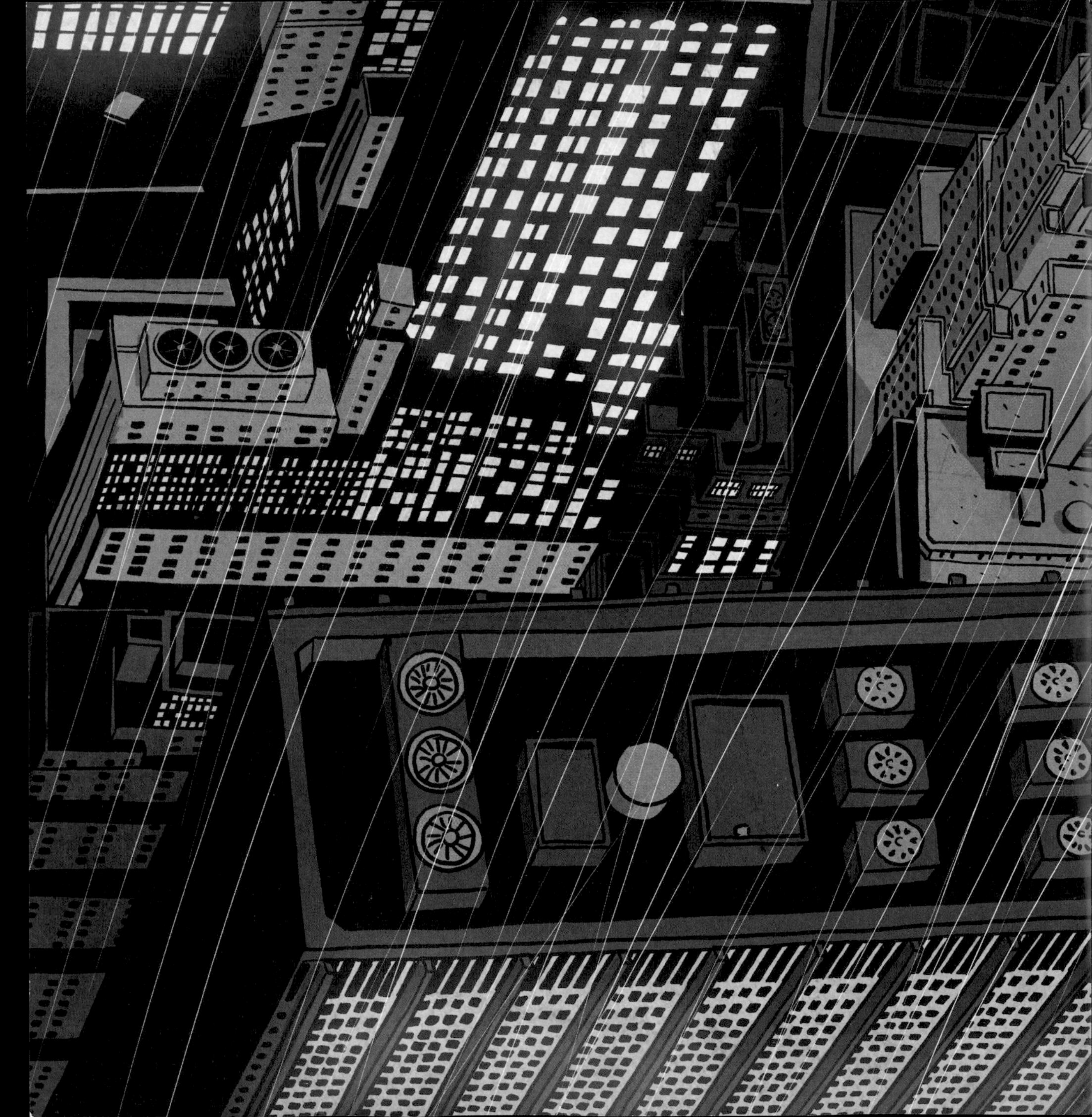

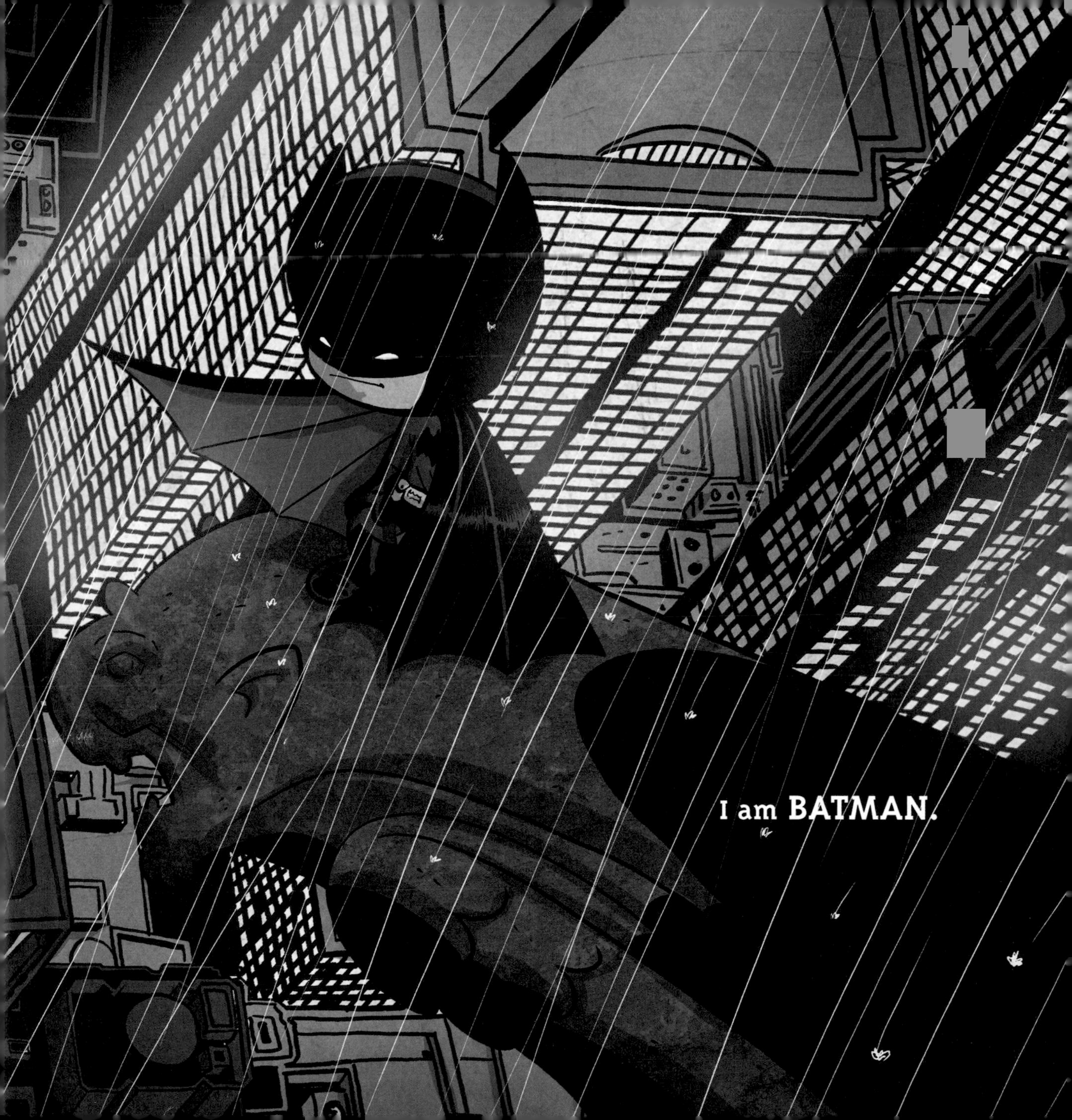

I am **BATMAN.**

I am also Bruce Wayne.

This is where I live, Gotham City.

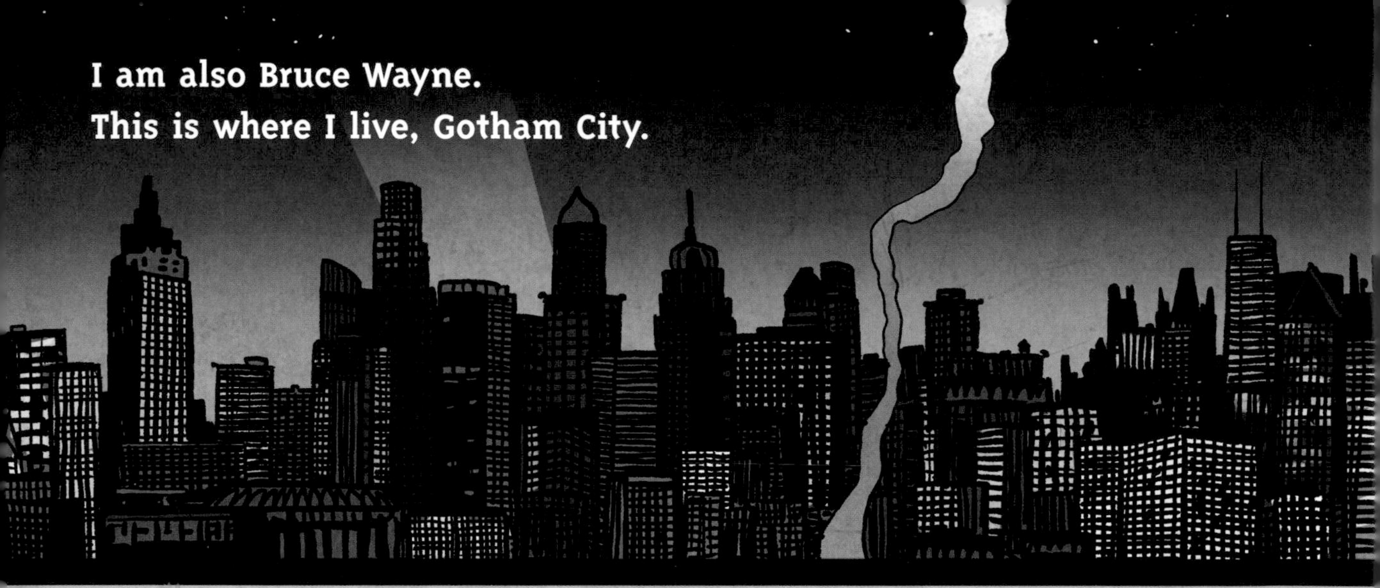

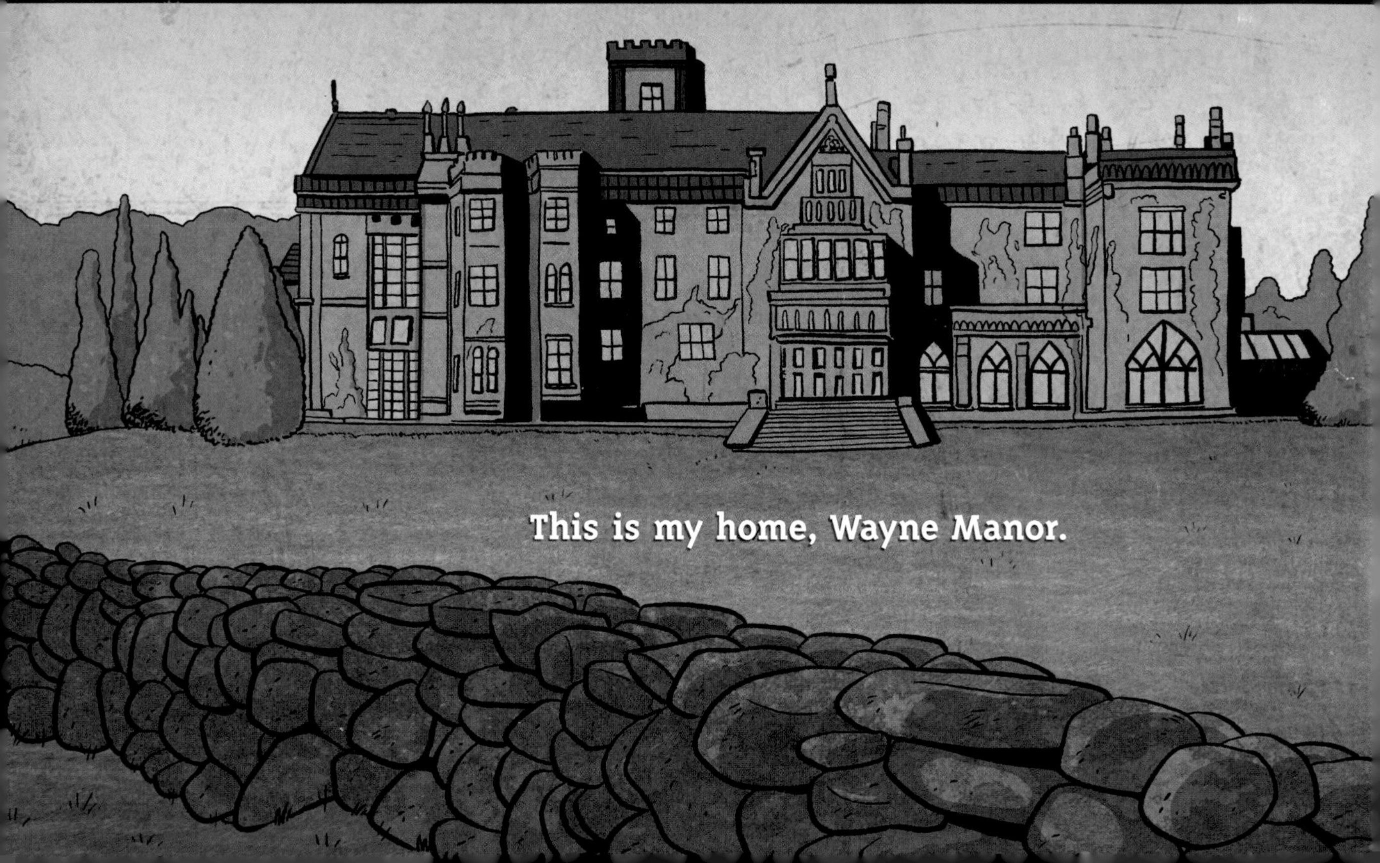

This is my home, Wayne Manor.

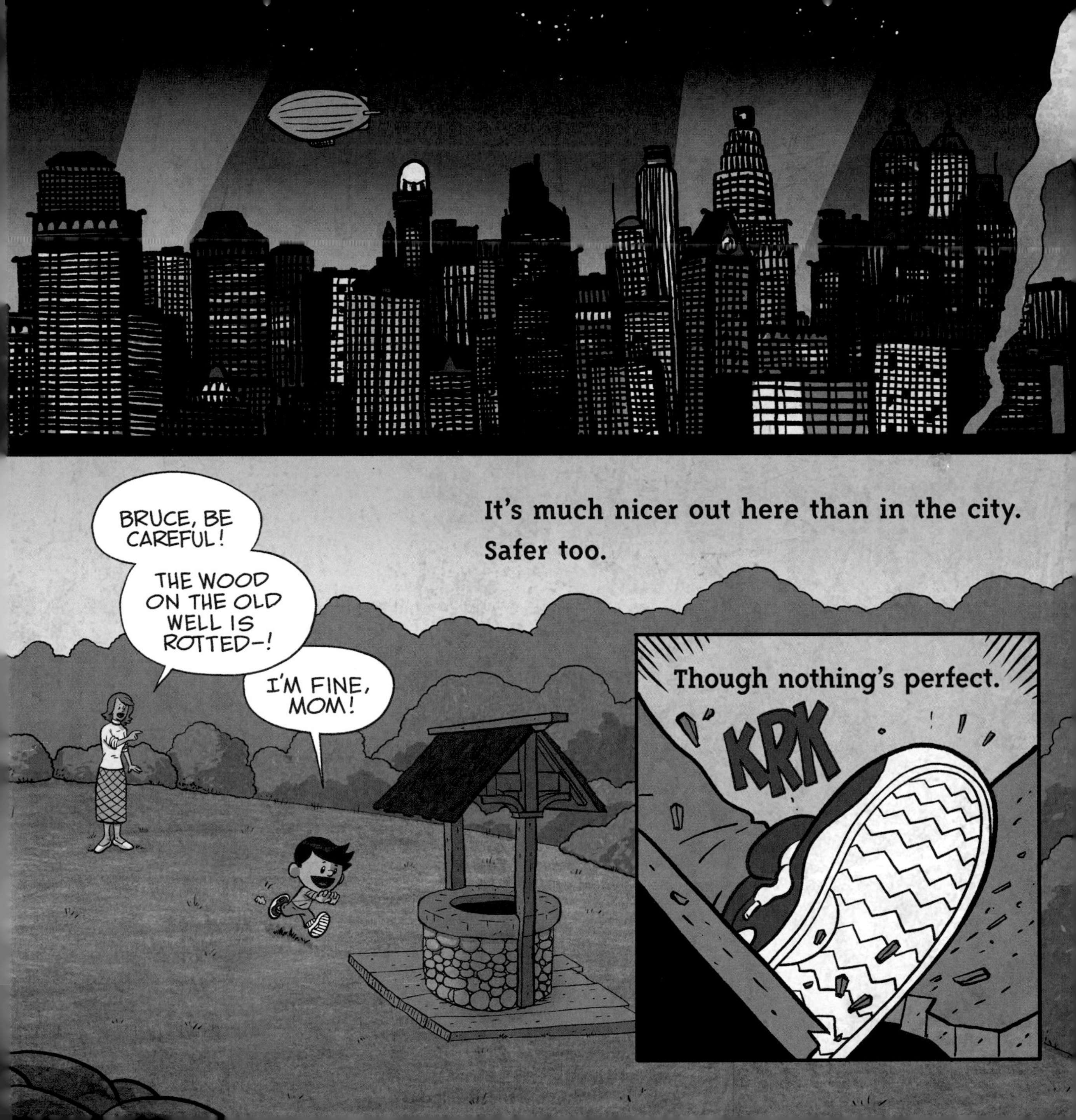
BRUCE, BE CAREFUL!
THE WOOD ON THE OLD WELL IS ROTTED-!
I'M FINE, MOM!
It's much nicer out here than in the city.
Safer too.
Though nothing's perfect.
KRK

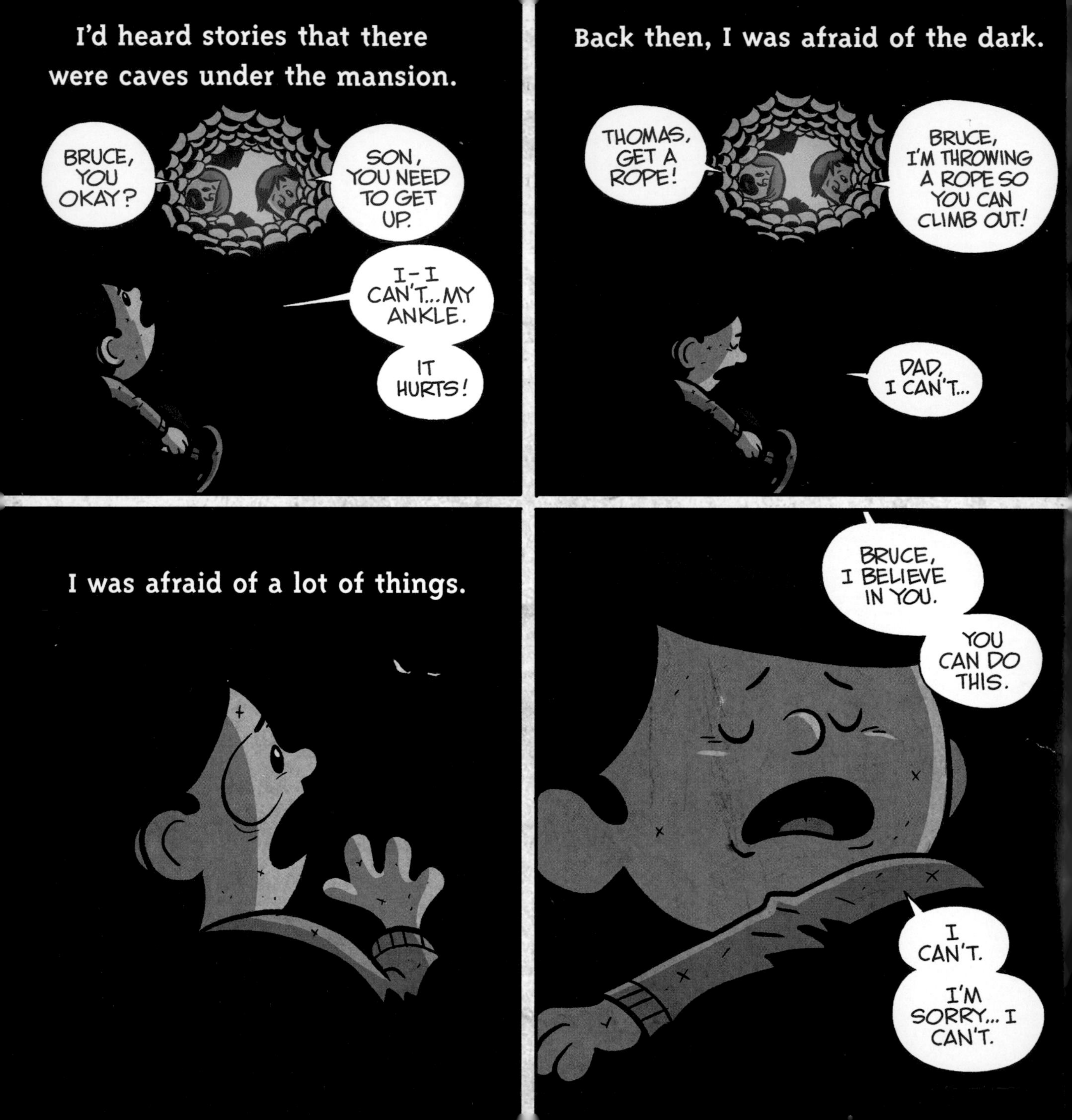
I'd heard stories that there were caves under the mansion.
BRUCE, YOU OKAY?
SON, YOU NEED TO GET UP.
I-I CAN'T... MY ANKLE.
IT HURTS!
Back then, I was afraid of the dark.
THOMAS, GET A ROPE!
BRUCE, I'M THROWING A ROPE SO YOU CAN CLIMB OUT!
DAD, I CAN'T...
I was afraid of a lot of things.
BRUCE, I BELIEVE IN YOU.
YOU CAN DO THIS.
I CAN'T.
I'M SORRY... I CAN'T.

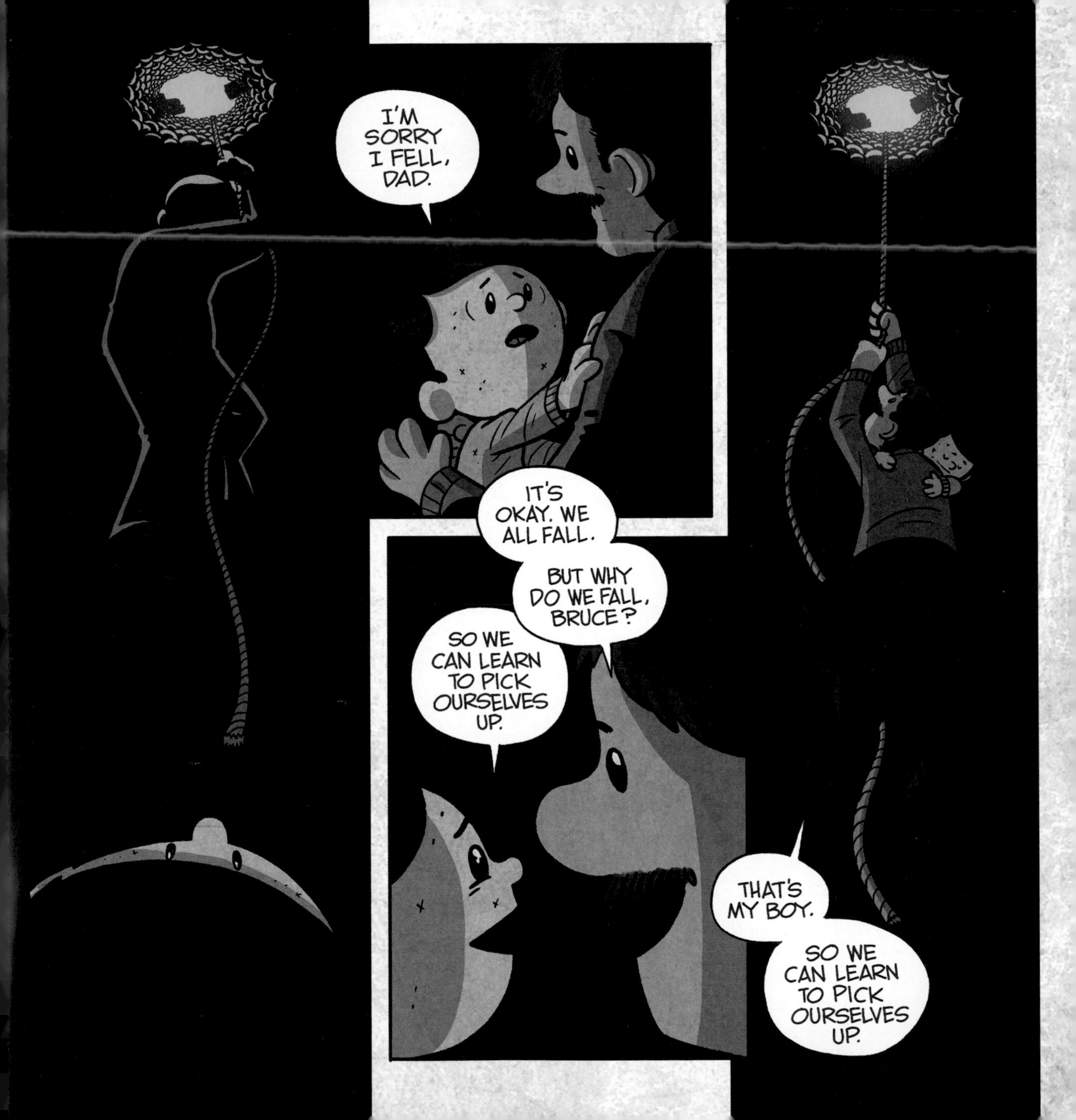
I'M SORRY I FELL, DAD.
IT'S OKAY. WE ALL FALL.
BUT WHY DO WE FALL, BRUCE?
SO WE CAN LEARN TO PICK OURSELVES UP.
THAT'S MY BOY.
SO WE CAN LEARN TO PICK OURSELVES UP.

When I was six years old, my parents took me to the movies.

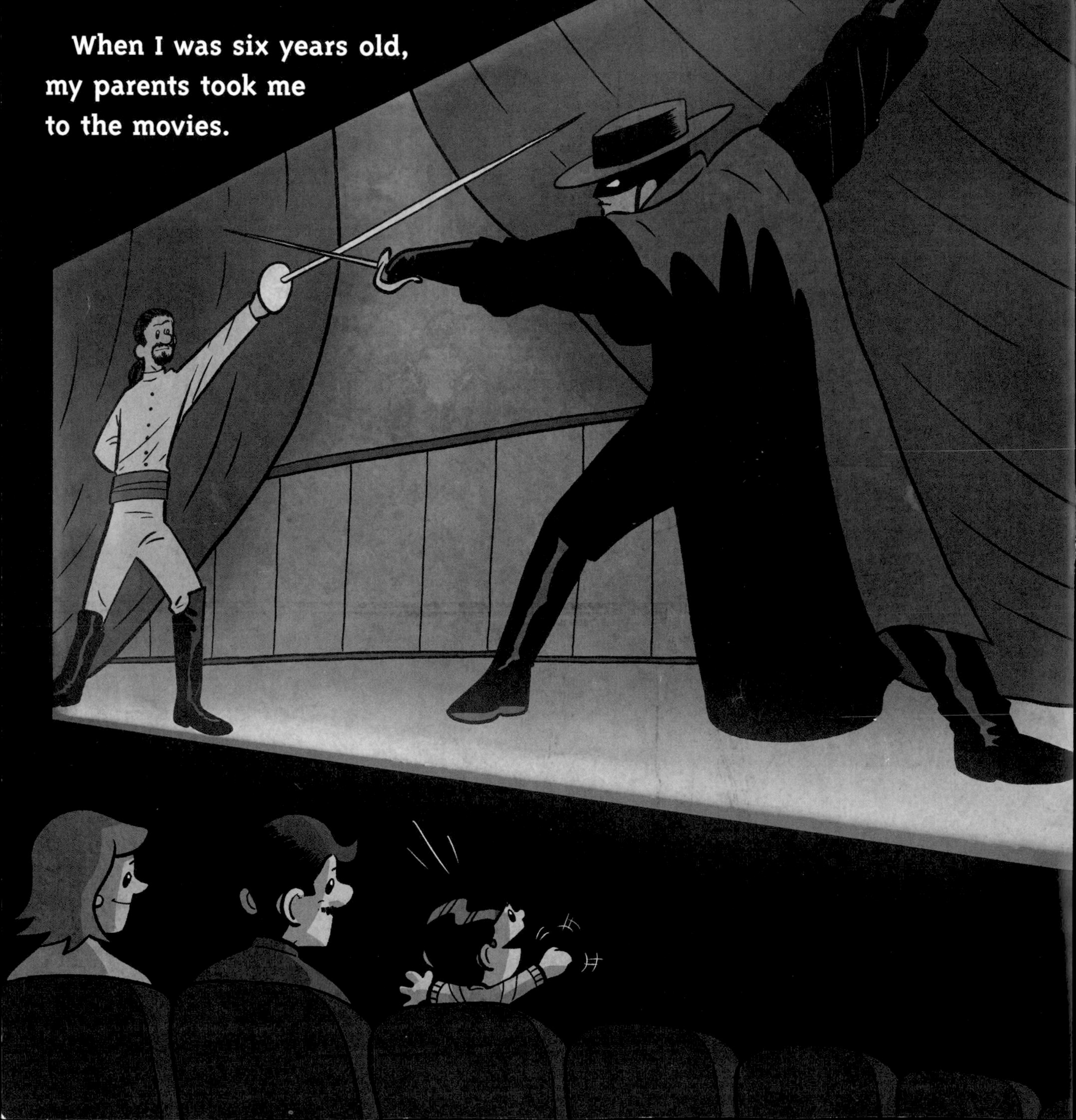

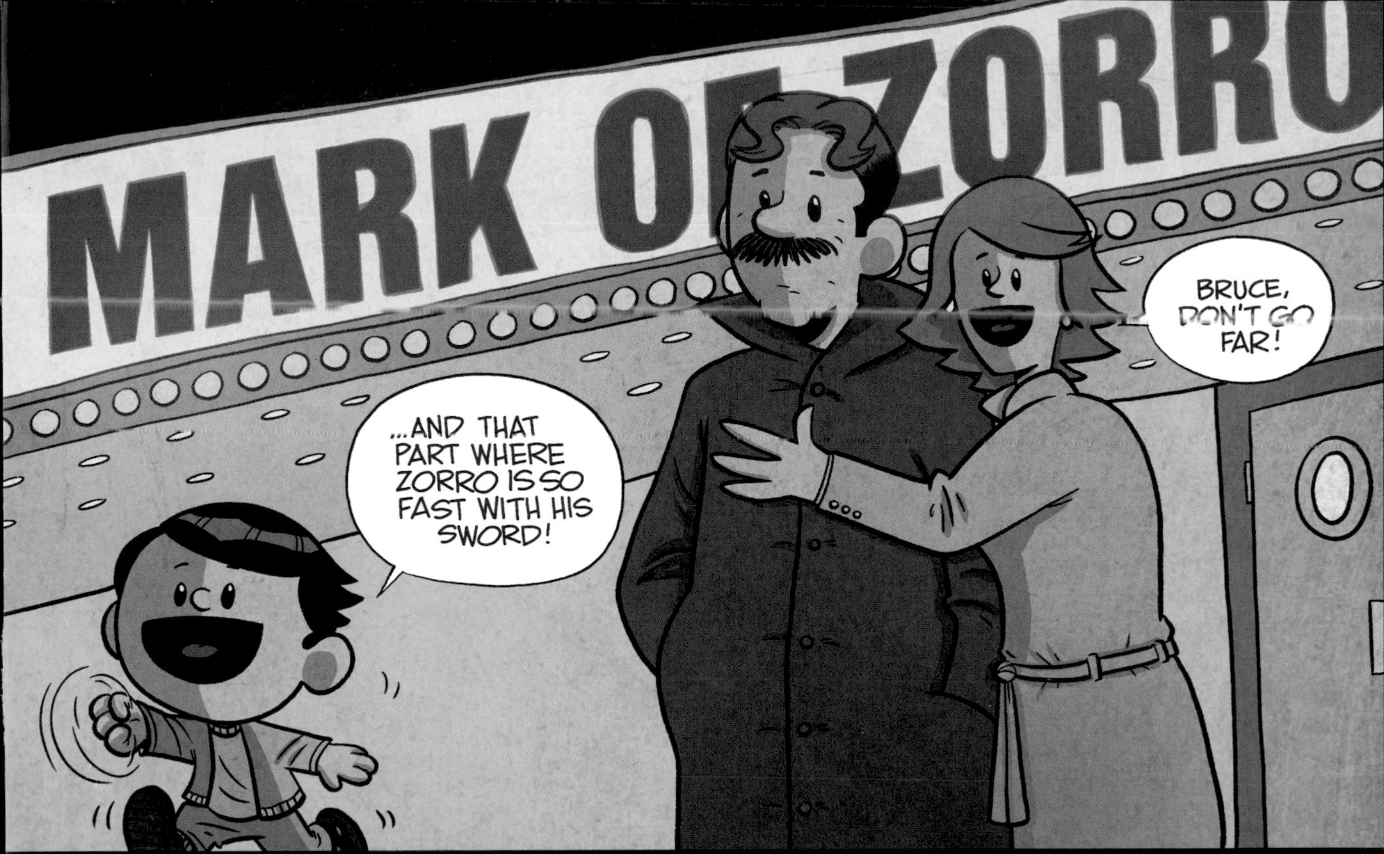
MARK OF ZORRO
...AND THAT PART WHERE ZORRO IS SO FAST WITH HIS SWORD!
BRUCE, DON'T GO FAR!

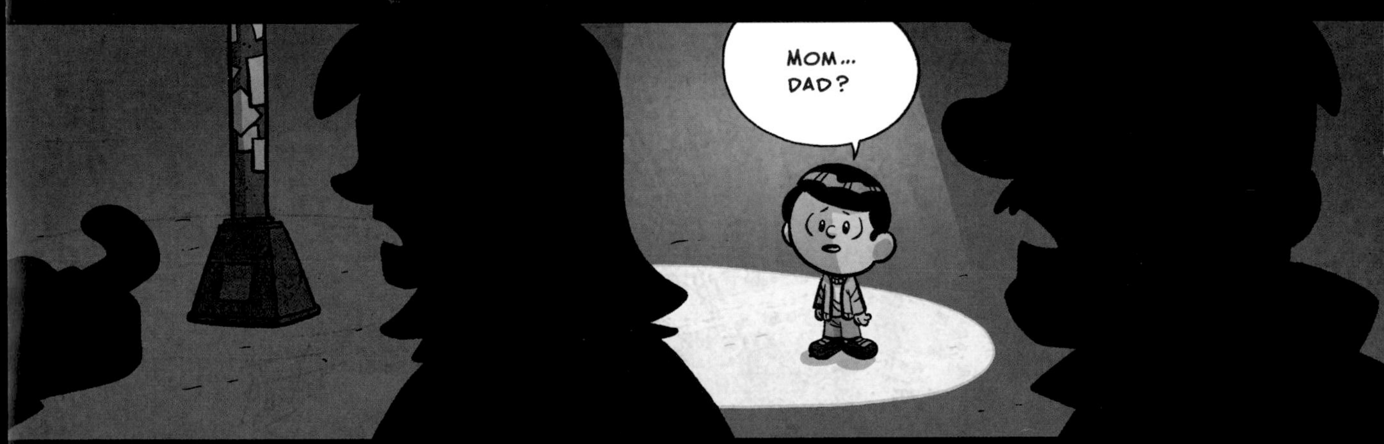
MOM... DAD?

In the alley, a criminal tried to rob my family.

That was the moment that changed my life.
The night my parents died.

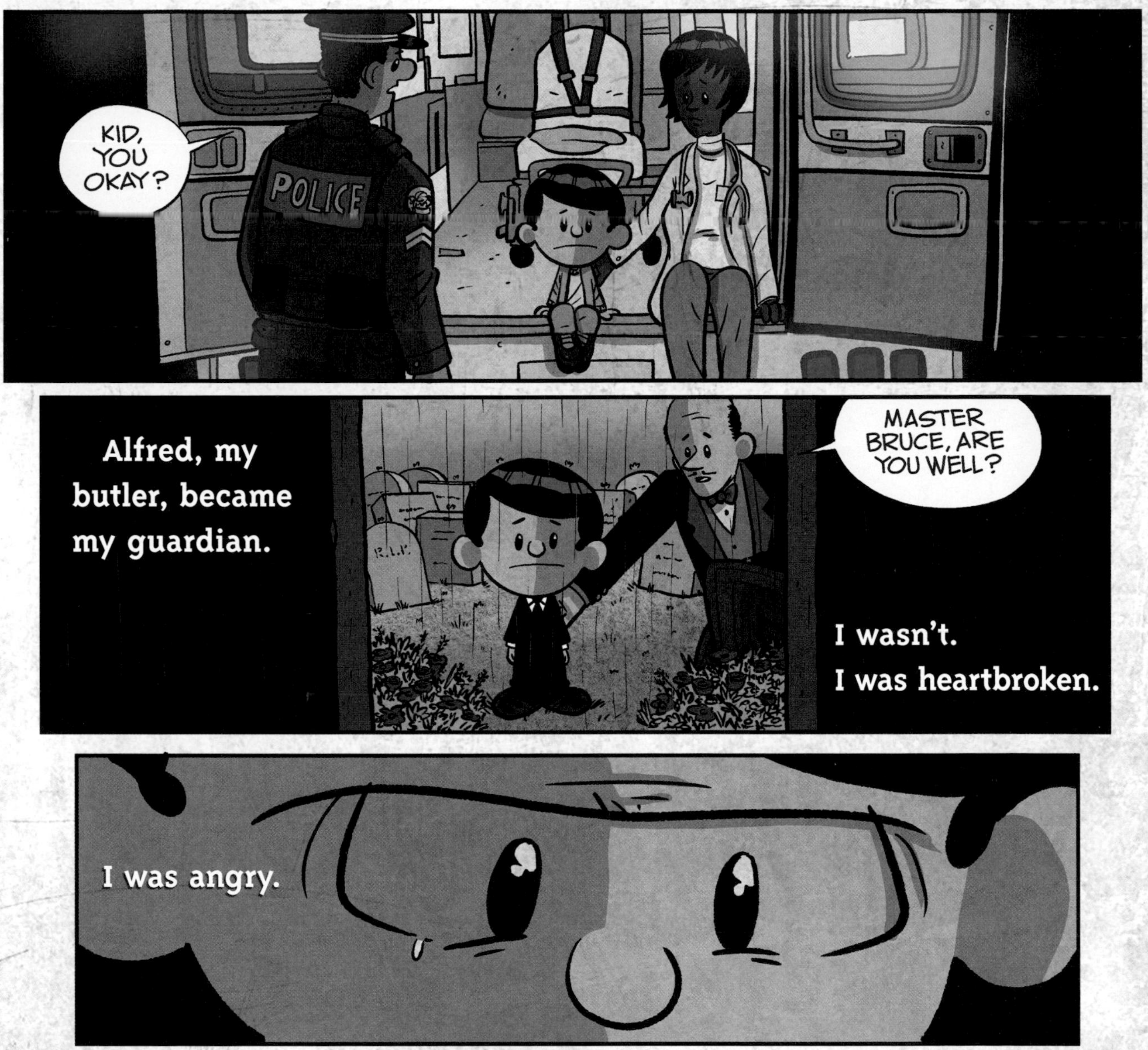
KID, YOU OKAY?
POLICE
Alfred, my butler, became my guardian.
MASTER BRUCE, ARE YOU WELL?
I wasn't.
I was heartbroken.
I was angry.

And most of all, I wanted to make sure that this never happened to anyone ever again.

By the time I was a teenager, I was already training: karate, tae kwon do, judo, and of course, boxing.

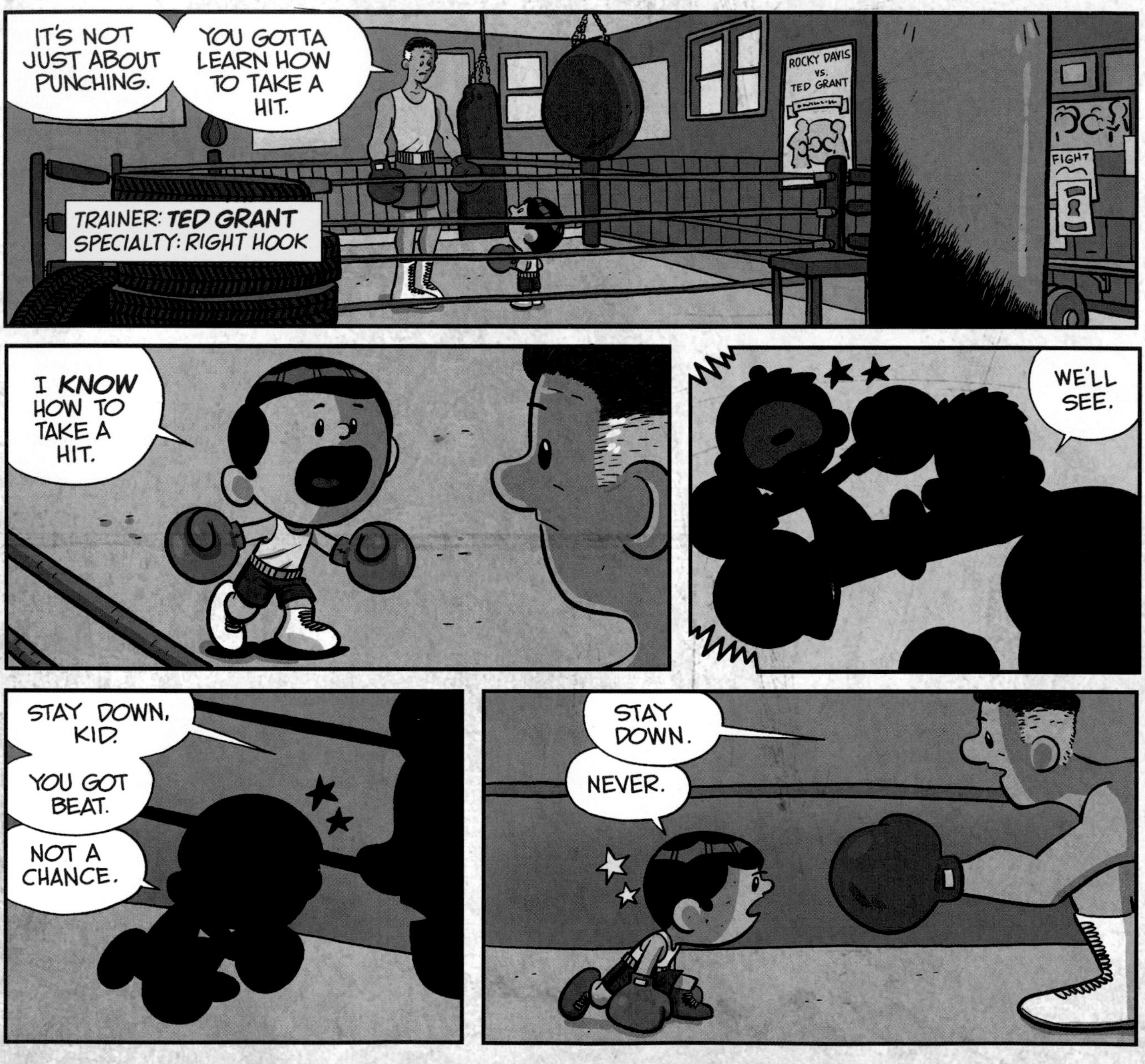
IT'S NOT JUST ABOUT PUNCHING.
YOU GOTTA LEARN HOW TO TAKE A HIT.
ROCKY DAVIS VS. TED GRANT
FIGHT
TRAINER: TED GRANT
SPECIALTY: RIGHT HOOK
I KNOW HOW TO TAKE A HIT.
WE'LL SEE.
STAY DOWN, KID.
YOU GOT BEAT.
NOT A CHANCE.
STAY DOWN.
NEVER.

Wherever the best teachers were, I found them.

Whatever the best tricks were, I learned them.

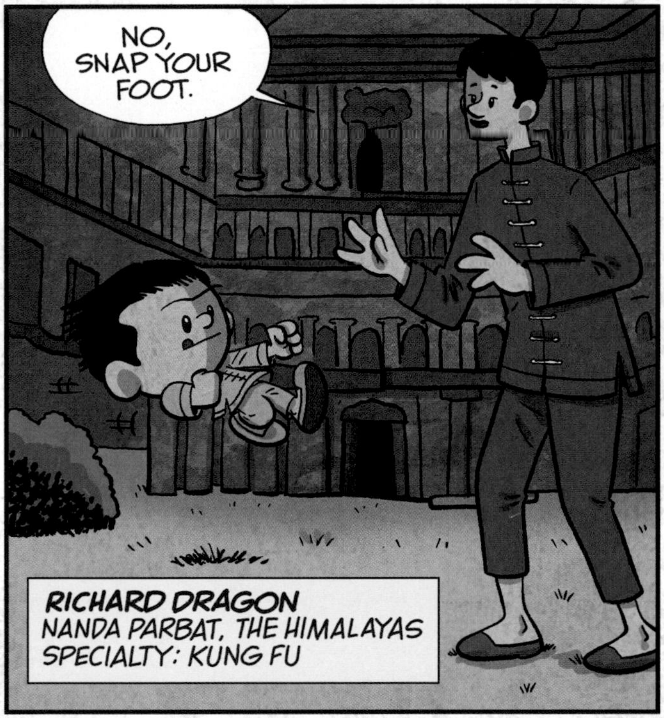
NO, SNAP YOUR FOOT.
RICHARD DRAGON
NANDA PARBAT, THE HIMALAYAS
SPECIALTY: KUNG FU

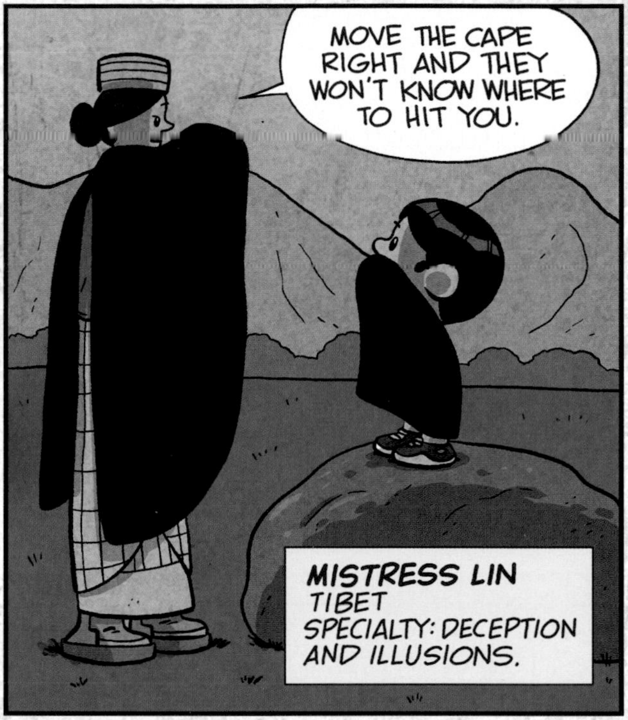
MOVE THE CAPE RIGHT AND THEY WON'T KNOW WHERE TO HIT YOU.
MISTRESS LIN
TIBET
SPECIALTY: DECEPTION AND ILLUSIONS.

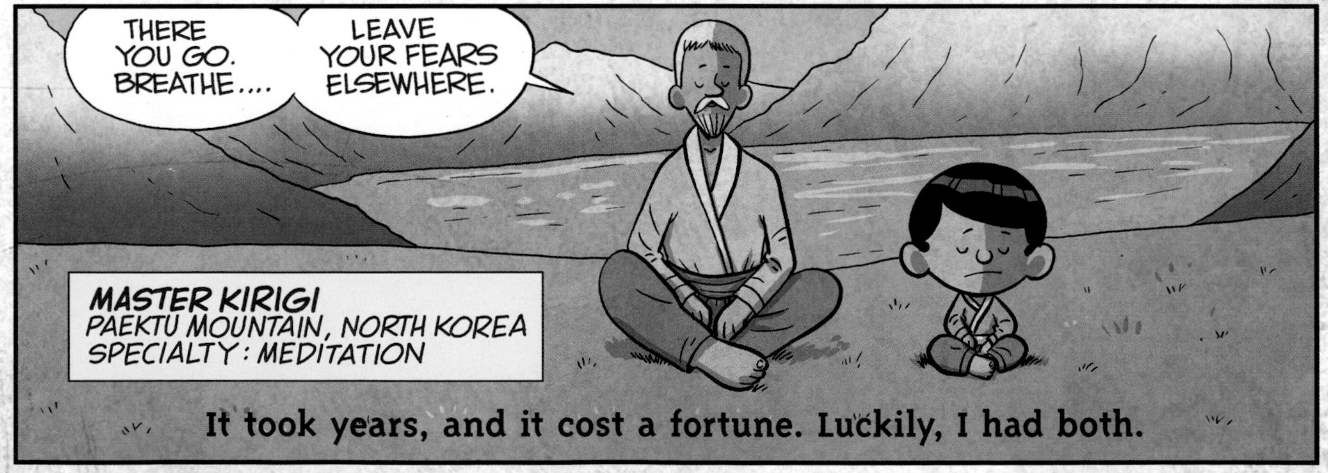
THERE YOU GO. BREATHE....
LEAVE YOUR FEARS ELSEWHERE.
MASTER KIRIGI
PAEKTU MOUNTAIN, NORTH KOREA
SPECIALTY: MEDITATION
It took years, and it cost a fortune. Luckily, I had both.

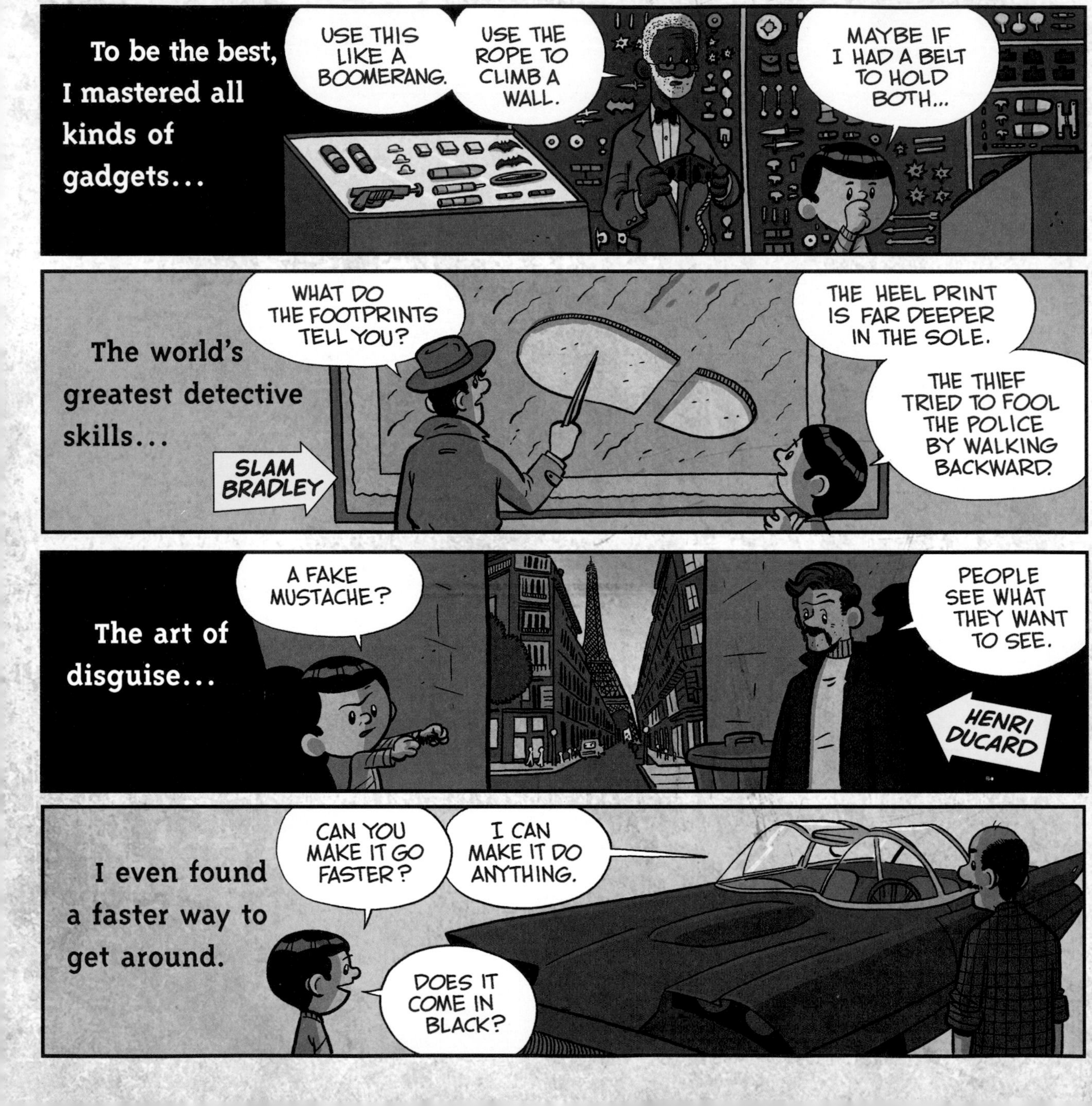

To be the best, I mastered all kinds of gadgets...
USE THIS LIKE A BOOMERANG.
USE THE ROPE TO CLIMB A WALL.
MAYBE IF I HAD A BELT TO HOLD BOTH...
The world's greatest detective skills...
SLAM BRADLEY
WHAT DO THE FOOTPRINTS TELL YOU?
THE HEEL PRINT IS FAR DEEPER IN THE SOLE.
THE THIEF TRIED TO FOOL THE POLICE BY WALKING BACKWARD.
The art of disguise...
A FAKE MUSTACHE?
PEOPLE SEE WHAT THEY WANT TO SEE.
HENRI DUCARD
I even found a faster way to get around.
CAN YOU MAKE IT GO FASTER?
I CAN MAKE IT DO ANYTHING.
DOES IT COME IN BLACK?

At twenty-five years old, I finally returned to Gotham City.
It wasn't hard to find trouble.

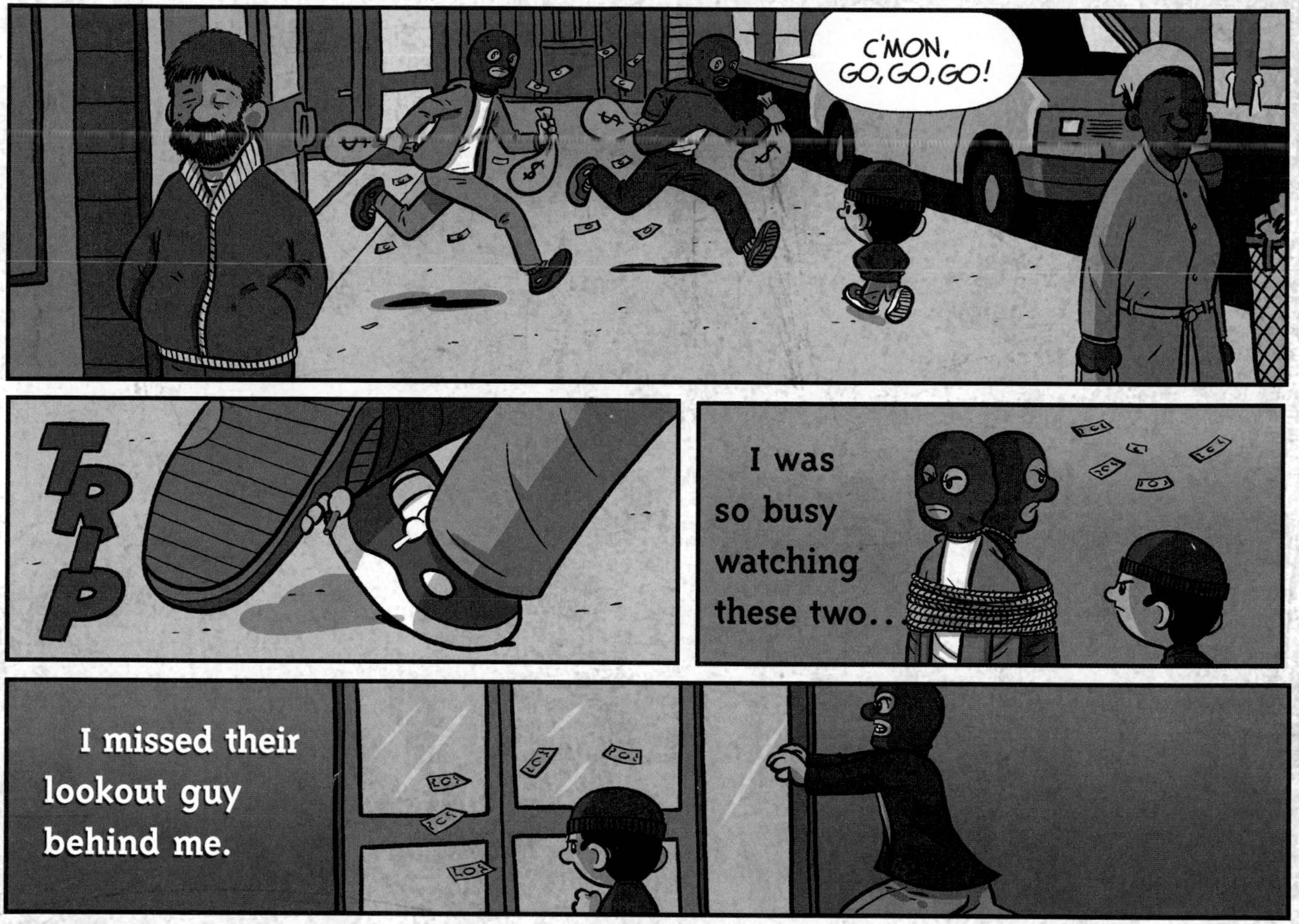
C'MON, GO, GO, GO!
TRIP
I was so busy watching these two...
I missed their lookout guy behind me.

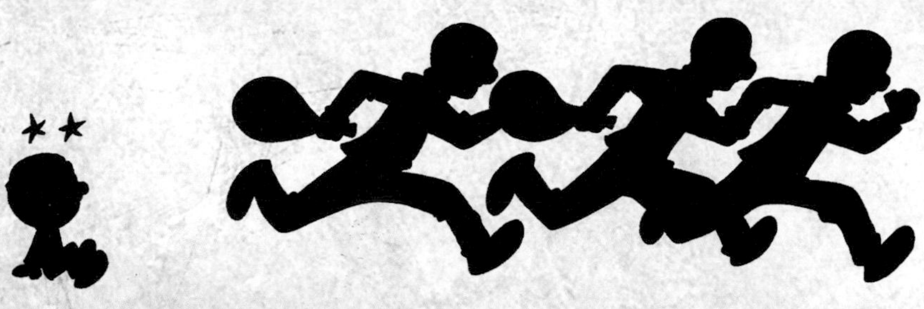

Another fall.
I thought my training was complete, but once again, the criminals won.

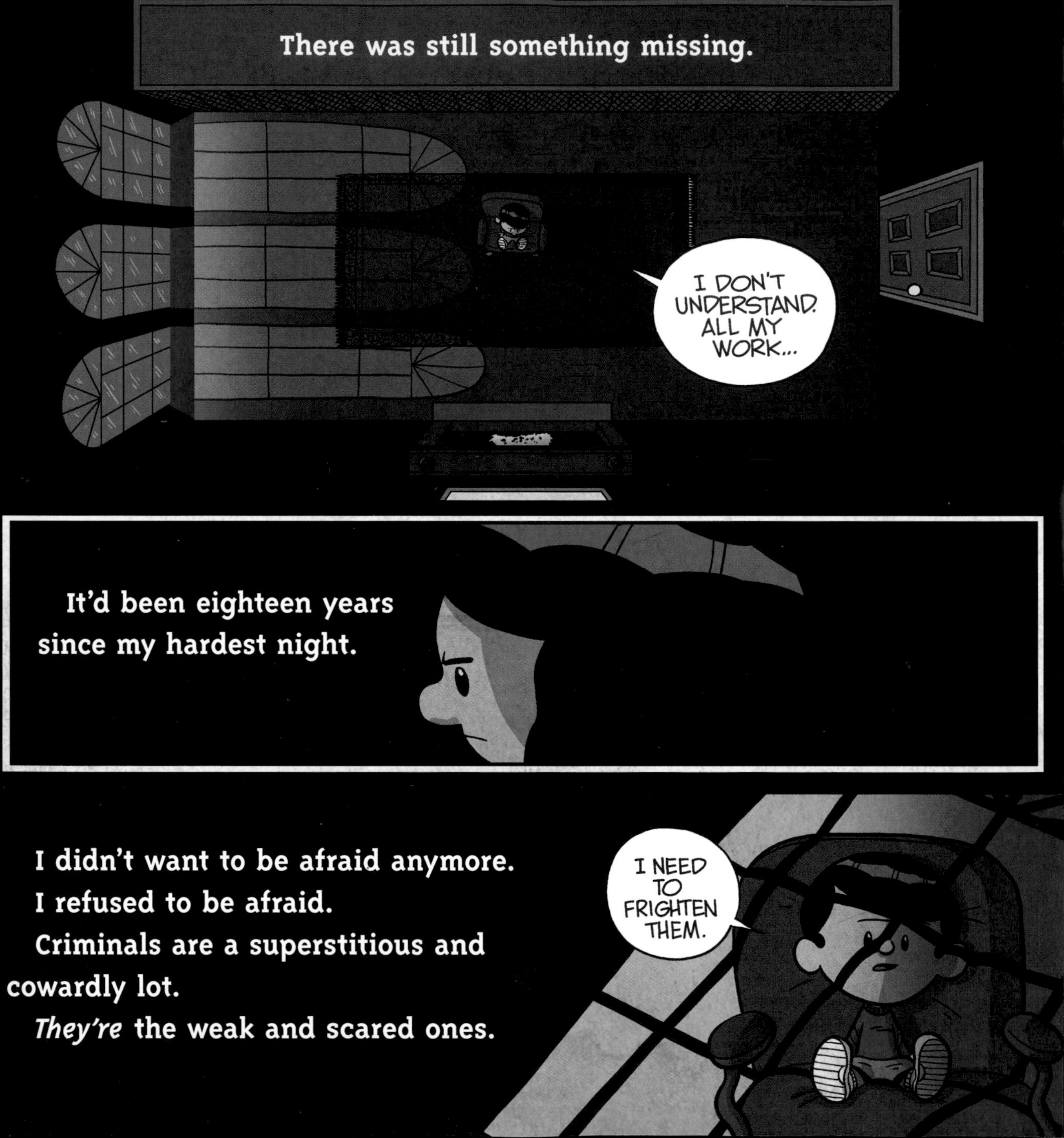

There was still something missing.

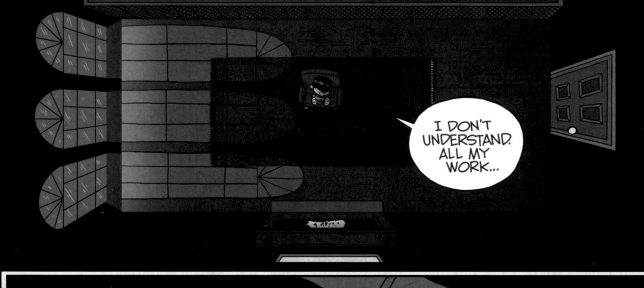

I DON'T UNDERSTAND. ALL MY WORK...

It'd been eighteen years since my hardest night.

I didn't want to be afraid anymore.
I refused to be afraid.
Criminals are a superstitious and cowardly lot.
They're the weak and scared ones.

I NEED TO FRIGHTEN THEM.

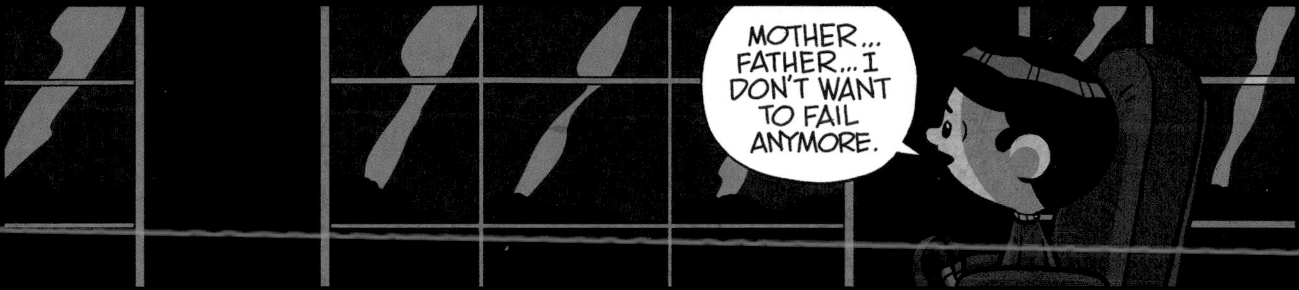
MOTHER... FATHER... I DON'T WANT TO FAIL ANYMORE.

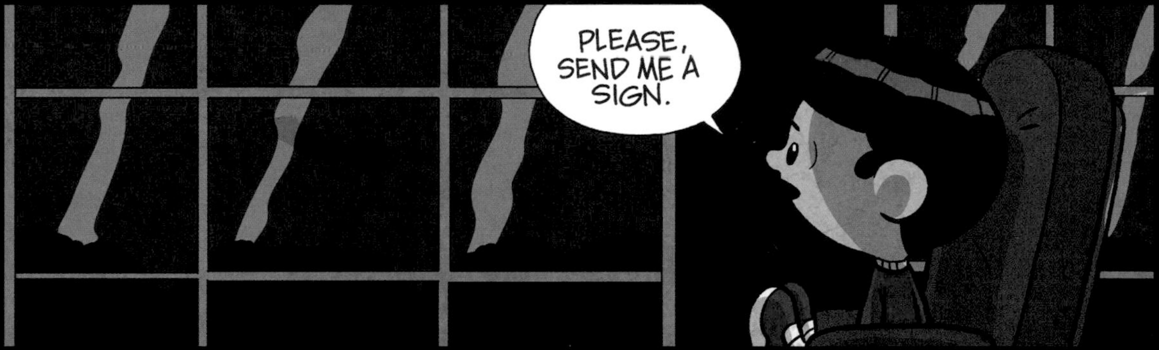
PLEASE, SEND ME A SIGN.

Suddenly, a creature crashed through the window.
I knew what it meant.

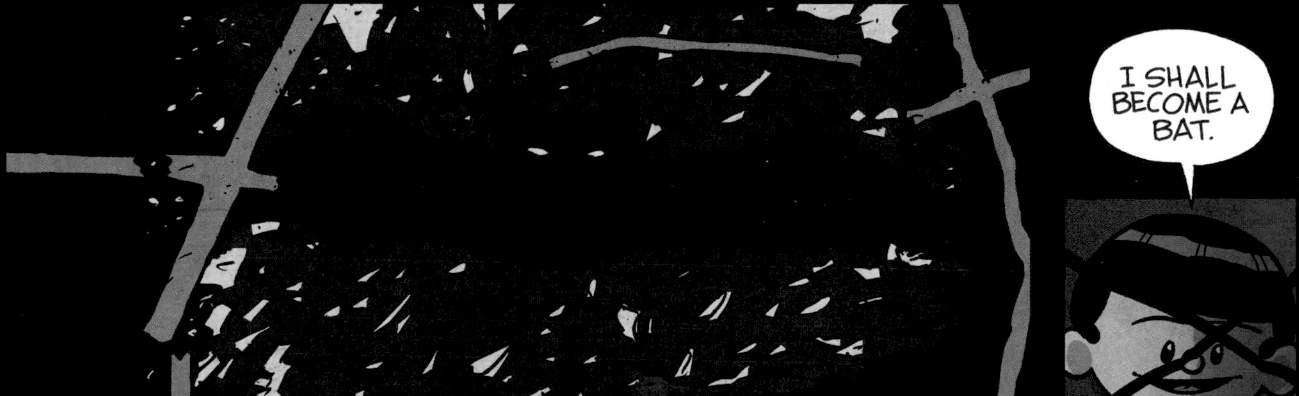
I SHALL BECOME A BAT.

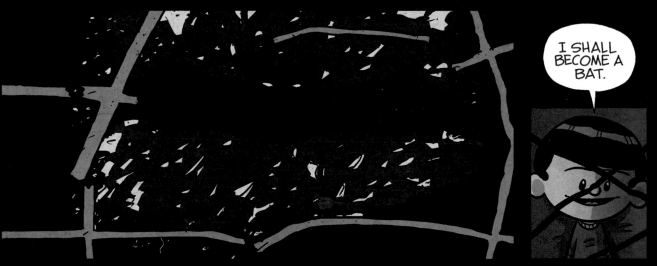

Finally, I was ready.

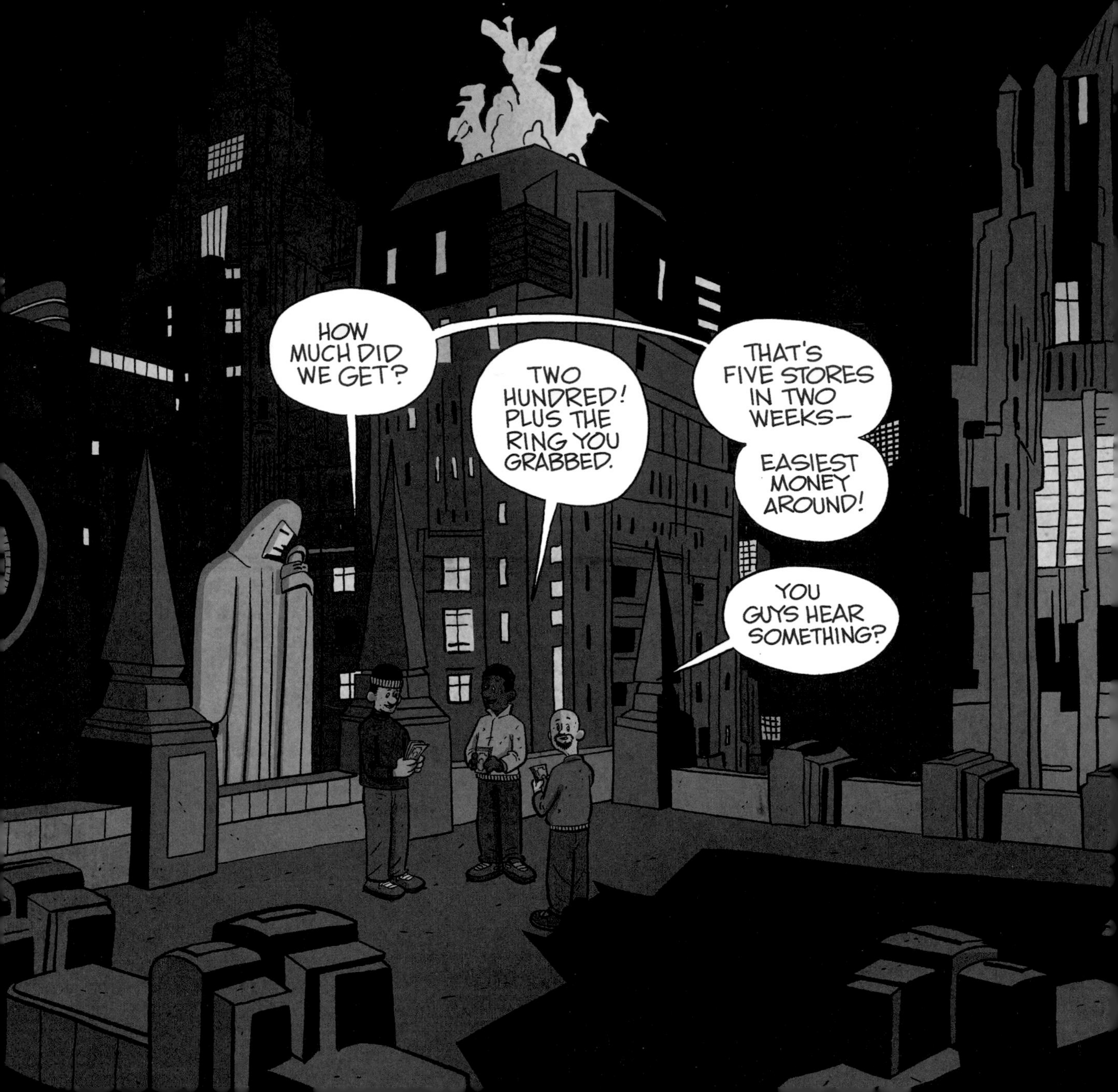
HOW MUCH DID WE GET?
TWO HUNDRED! PLUS THE RING YOU GRABBED.
THAT'S FIVE STORES IN TWO WEEKS–
EASIEST MONEY AROUND!
YOU GUYS HEAR SOMETHING?

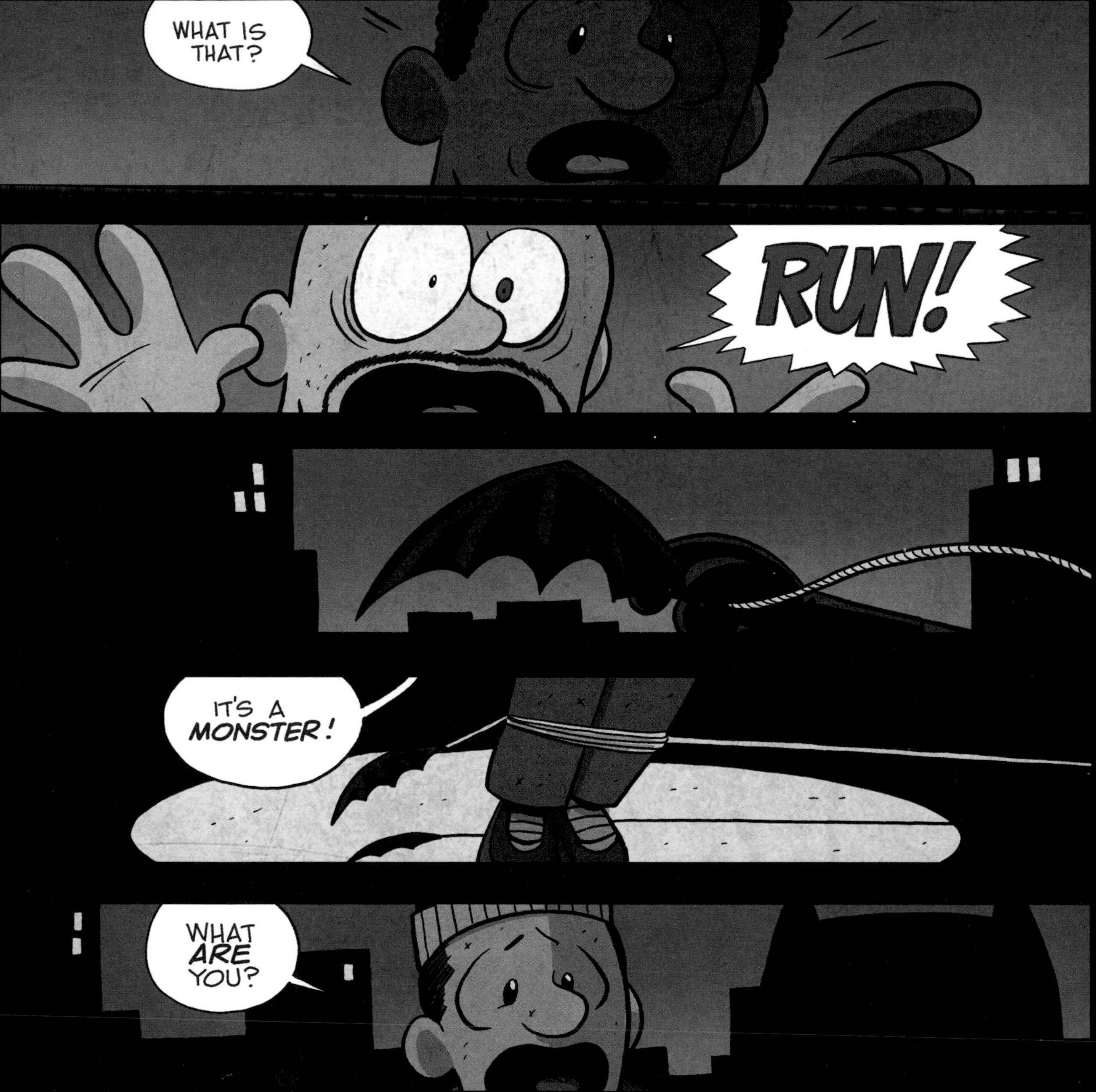
WHAT IS THAT?
RUN!
IT'S A MONSTER!
WHAT ARE YOU?

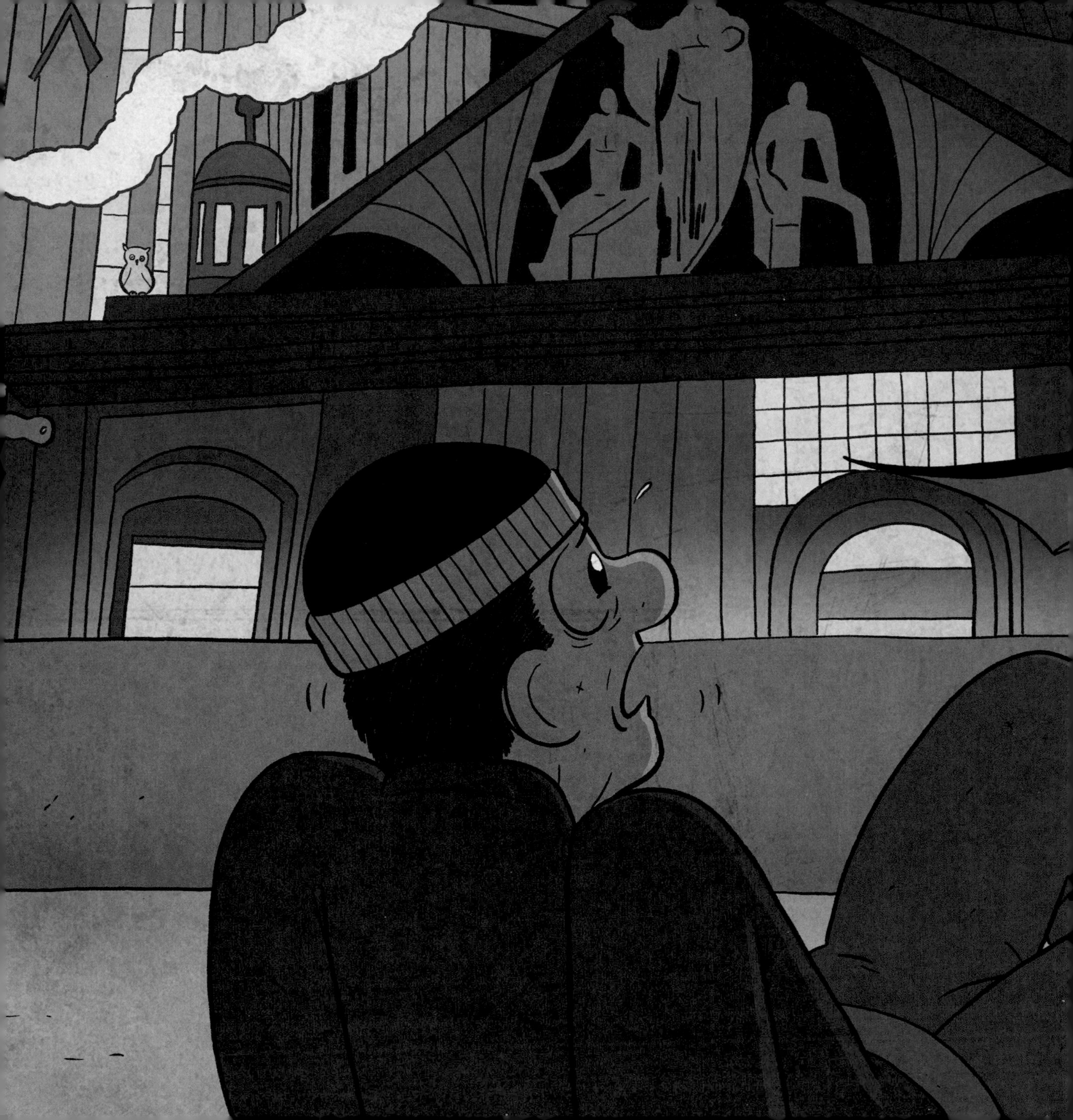

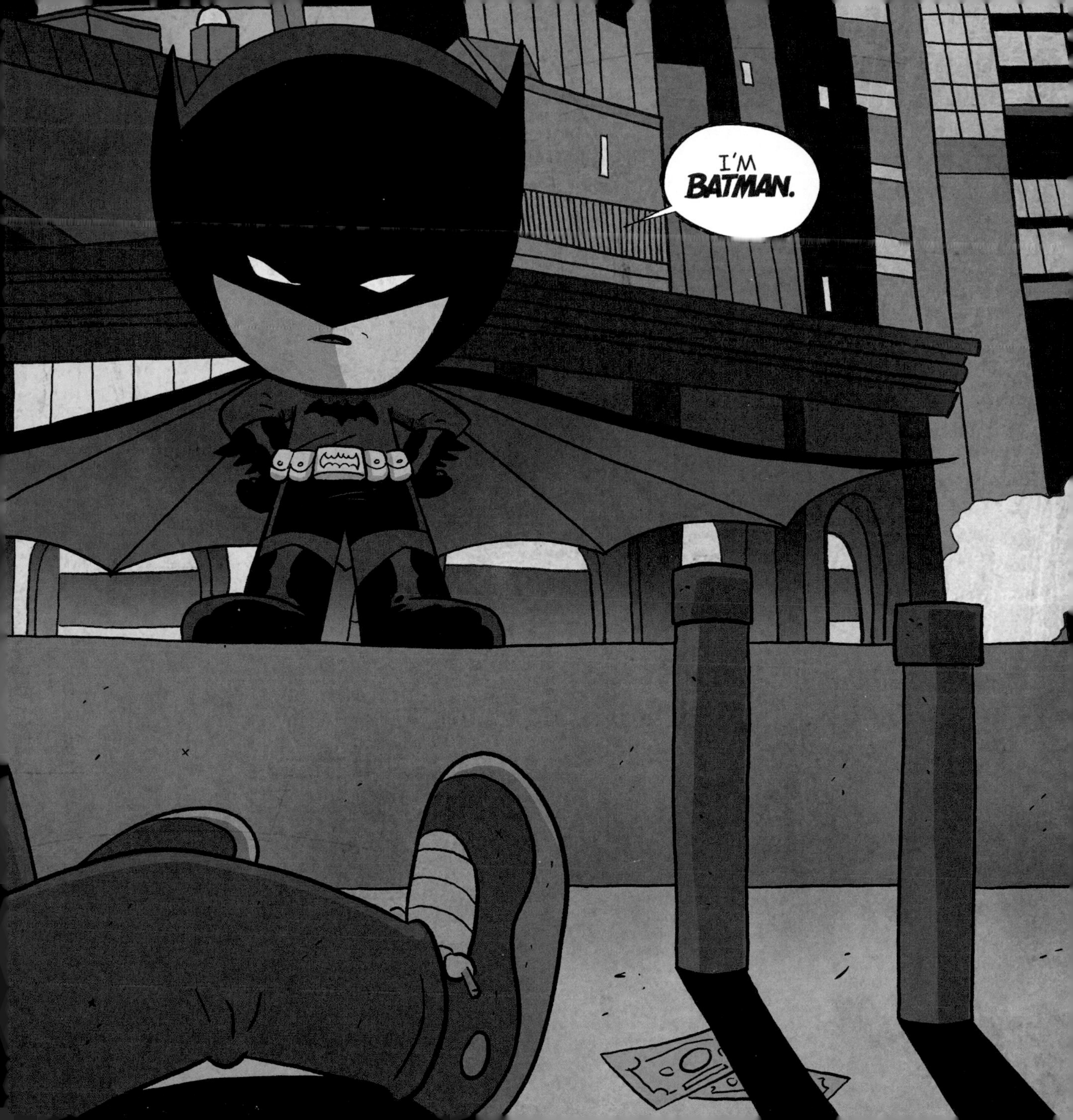
I'M BATMAN.

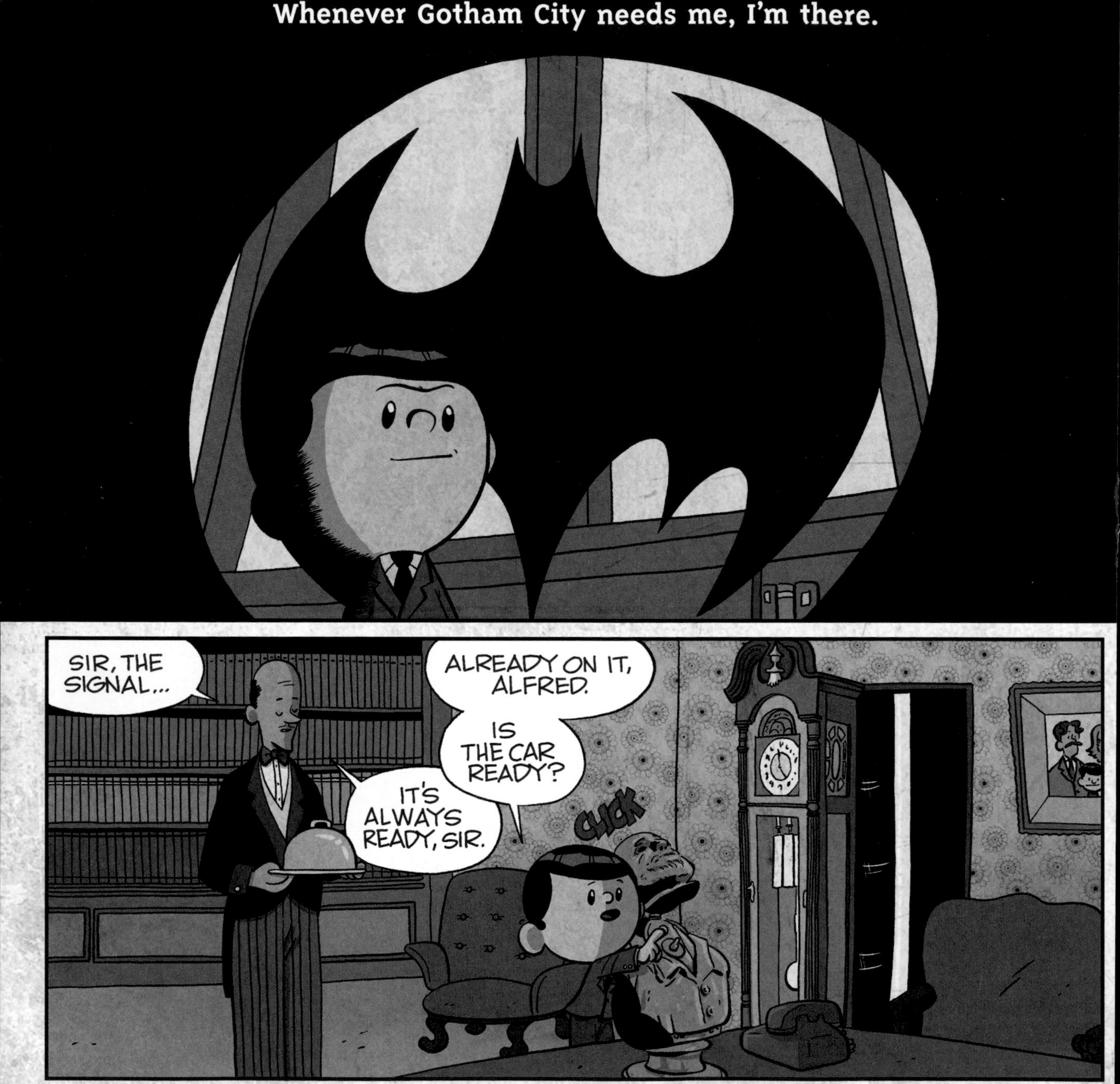
Whenever Gotham City needs me, I'm there.
SIR, THE SIGNAL...
ALREADY ON IT, ALFRED.
IS THE CAR READY?
IT'S ALWAYS READY, SIR.
CLICK

I've got the best tools...

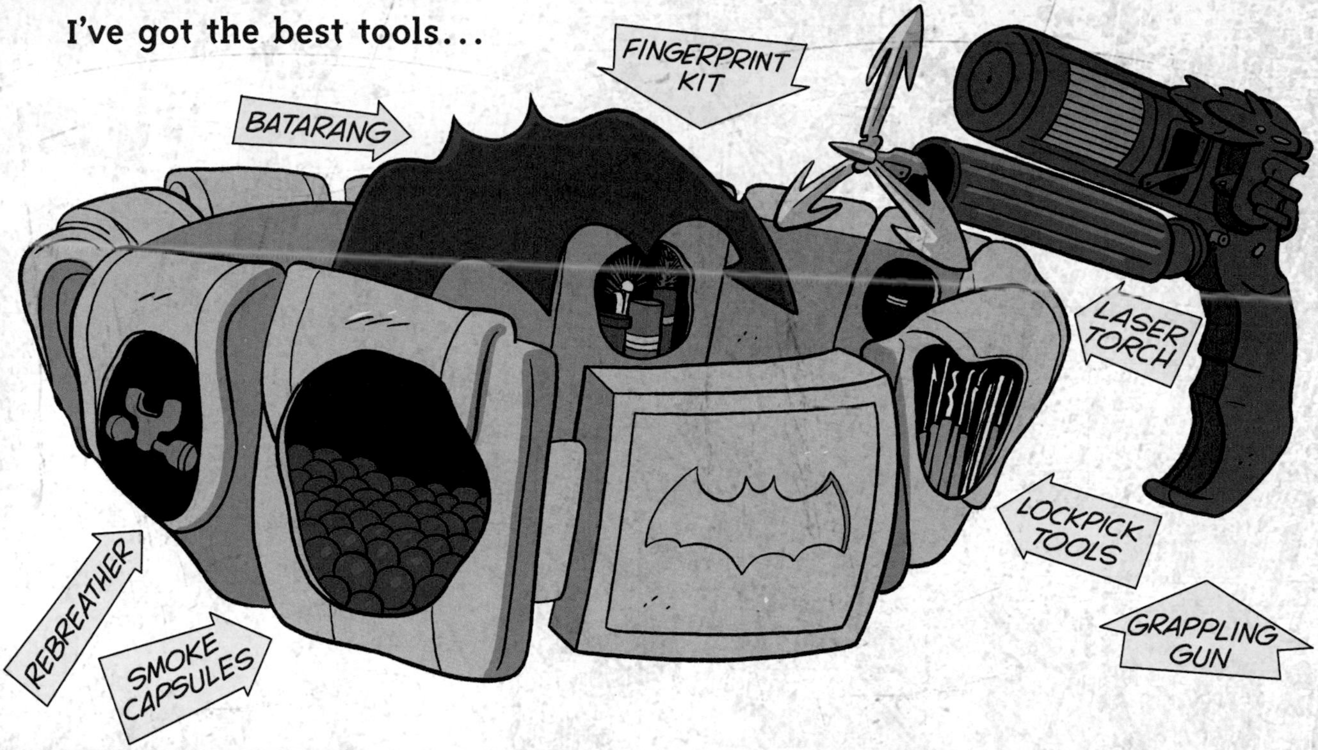
FINGERPRINT KIT
BATARANG
LASER TORCH
LOCKPICK TOOLS
GRAPPLING GUN
REBREATHER
SMOKE CAPSULES

The best gadgets...

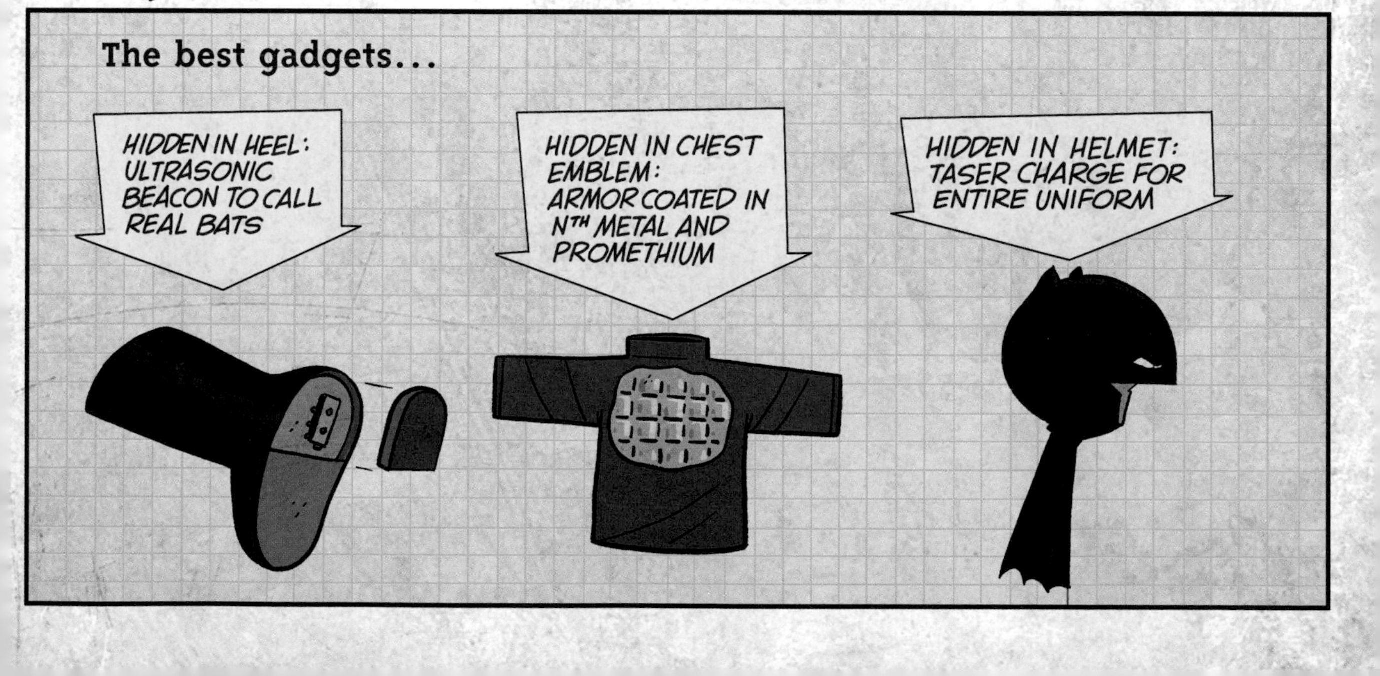
HIDDEN IN HEEL: ULTRASONIC BEACON TO CALL REAL BATS
HIDDEN IN CHEST EMBLEM: ARMOR COATED IN NTH METAL AND PROMETHIUM
HIDDEN IN HELMET: TASER CHARGE FOR ENTIRE UNIFORM

And the most wonderful toys.

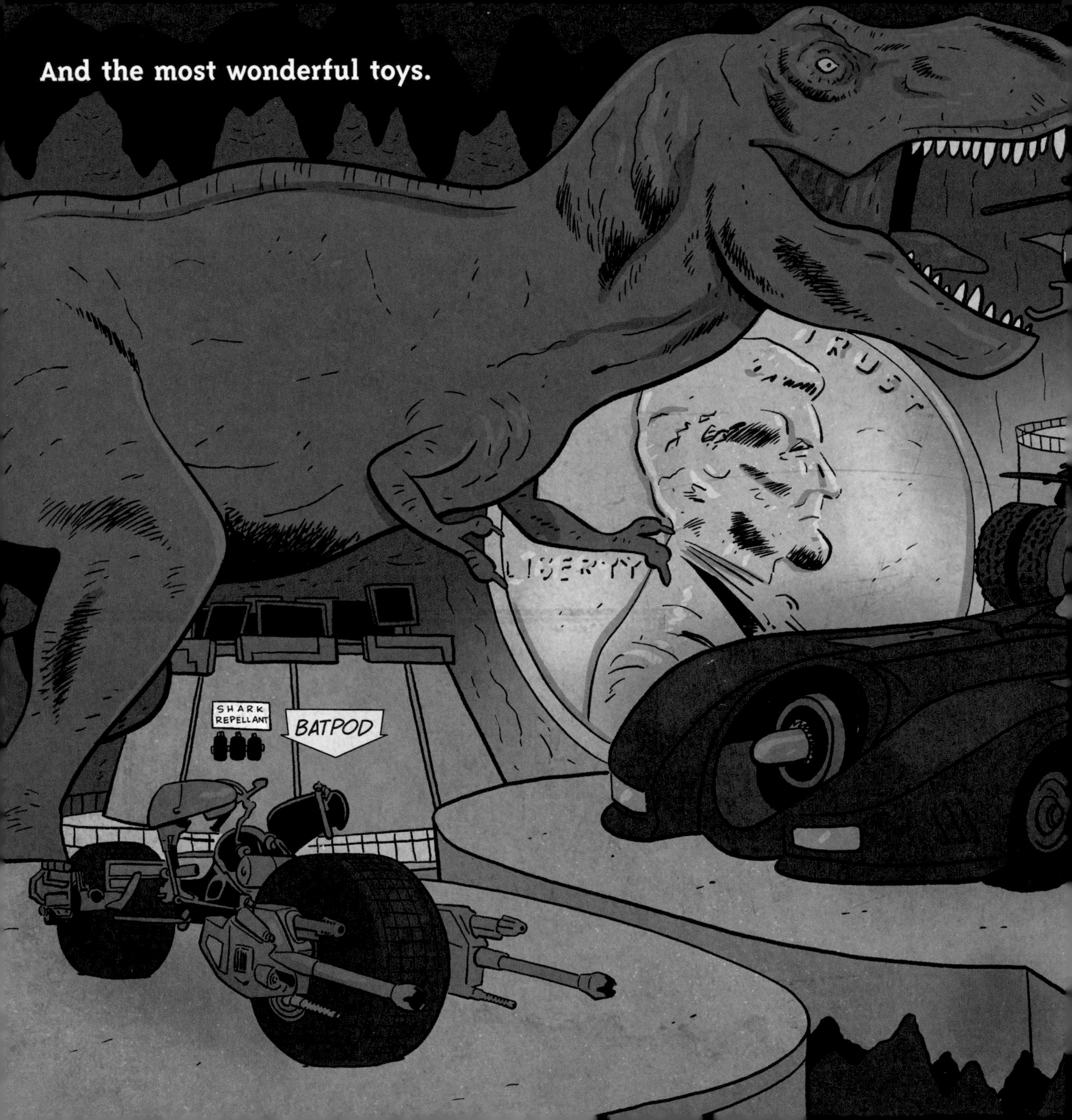
TRUST
LIBERTY
SHARK
REPELLANT
BATPOD

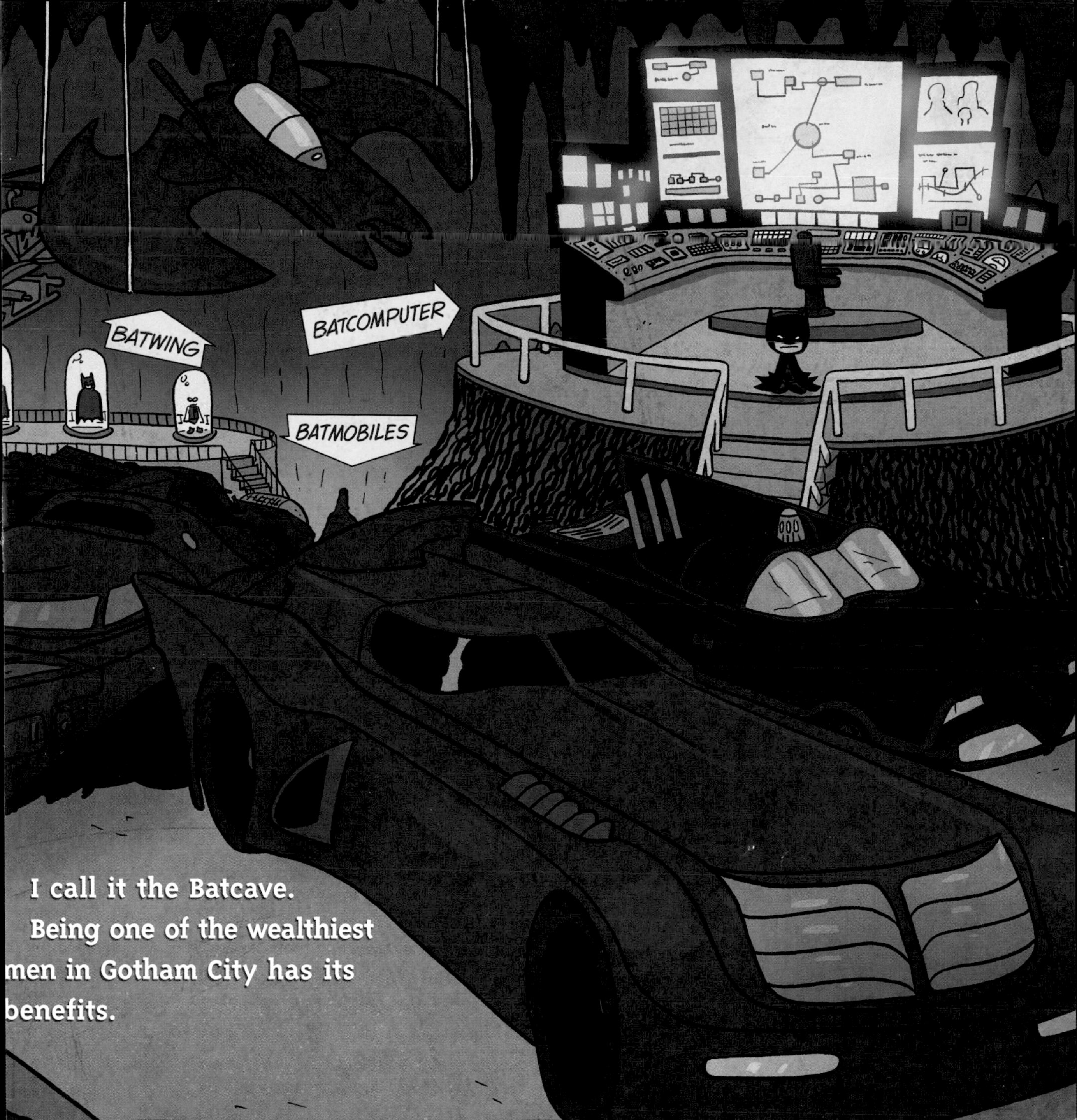
BATWING
BATCOMPUTER
BATMOBILES

I call it the Batcave.
Being one of the wealthiest men in Gotham City has its benefits.

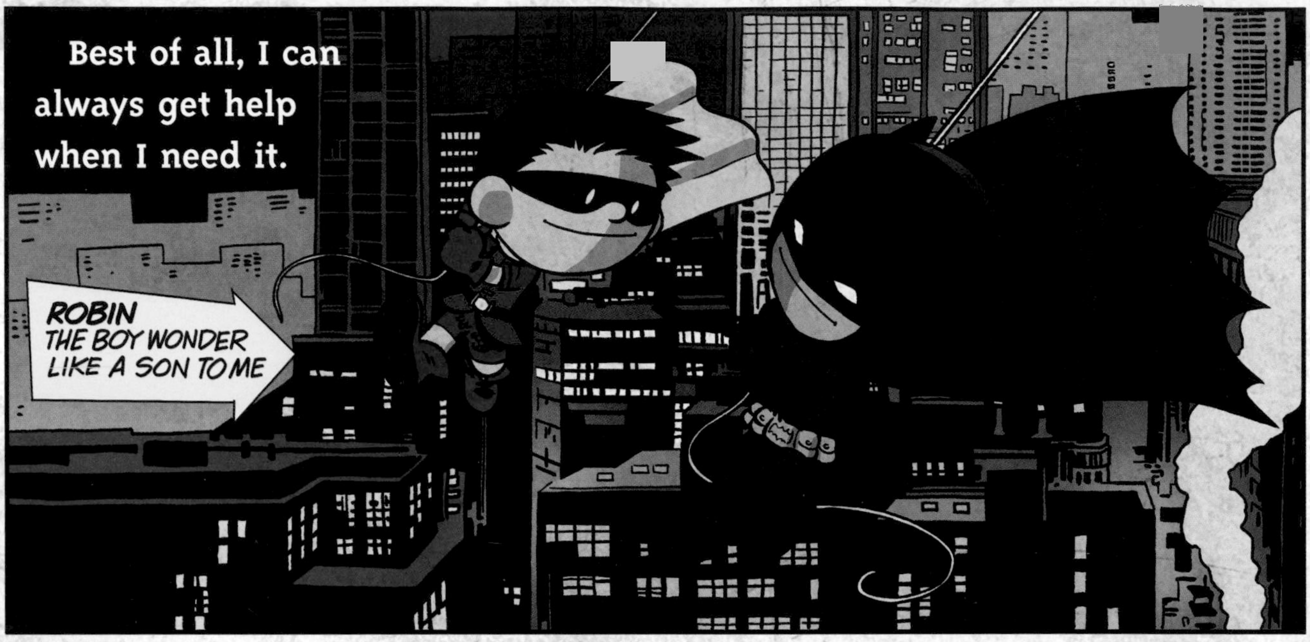
Best of all, I can always get help when I need it.
ROBIN
THE BOY WONDER
LIKE A SON TO ME

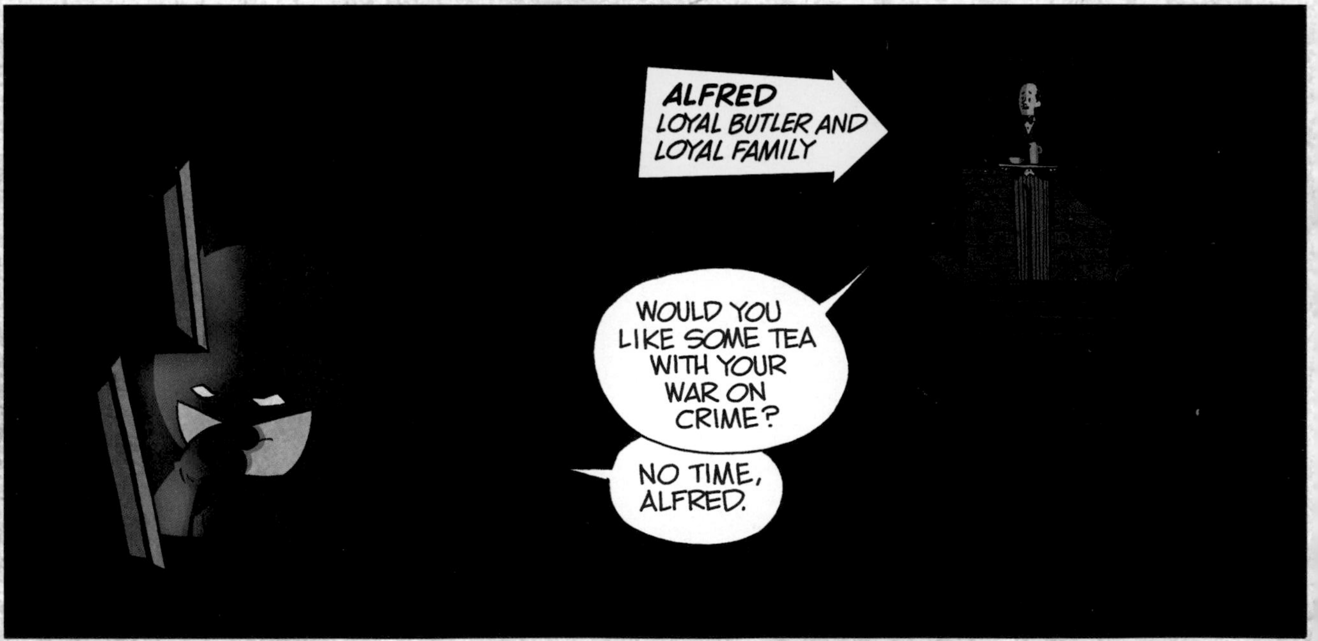
ALFRED
LOYAL BUTLER AND
LOYAL FAMILY
WOULD YOU LIKE SOME TEA WITH YOUR WAR ON CRIME?
NO TIME, ALFRED.

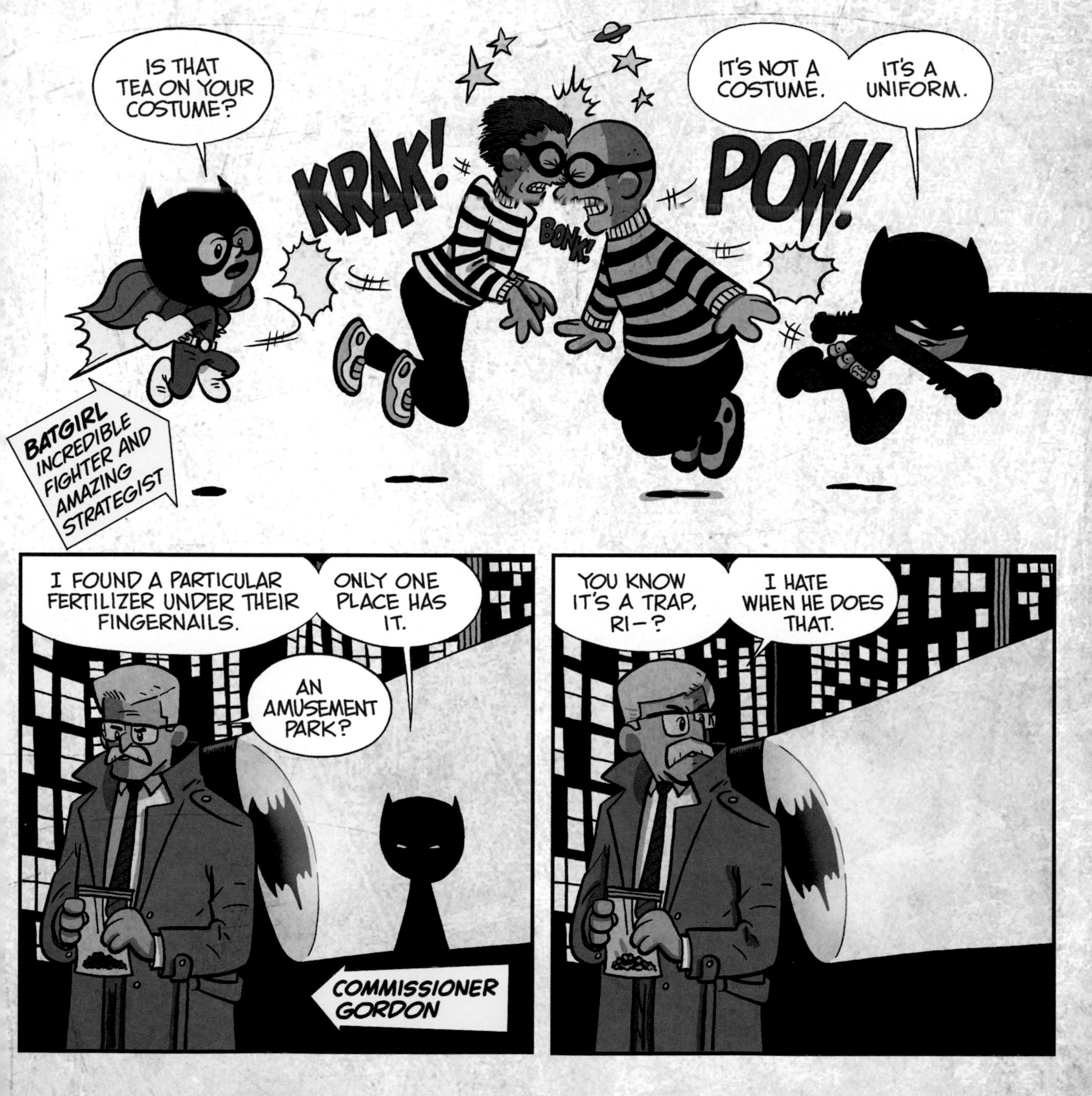
IS THAT TEA ON YOUR COSTUME?
KRAK!
BONK!
POW!
IT'S NOT A COSTUME.
IT'S A UNIFORM.
BATGIRL INCREDIBLE FIGHTER AND AMAZING STRATEGIST
I FOUND A PARTICULAR FERTILIZER UNDER THEIR FINGERNAILS.
ONLY ONE PLACE HAS IT.
AN AMUSEMENT PARK?
COMMISSIONER GORDON
YOU KNOW IT'S A TRAP, RI—?
I HATE WHEN HE DOES THAT.

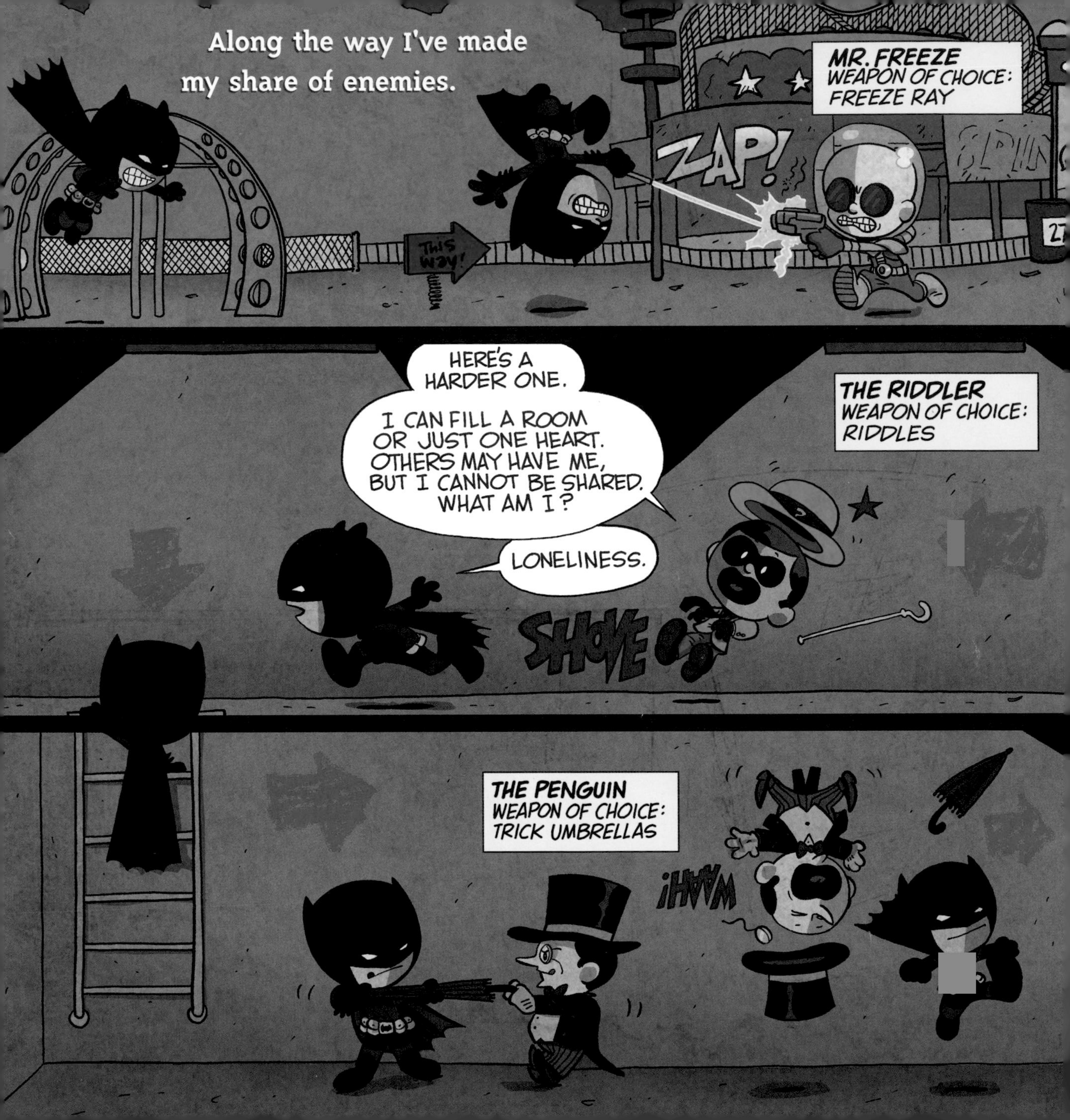
Along the way I've made my share of enemies.
THIS WAY!
ZAP!
MR. FREEZE
WEAPON OF CHOICE: FREEZE RAY
HERE'S A HARDER ONE.
I CAN FILL A ROOM OR JUST ONE HEART. OTHERS MAY HAVE ME, BUT I CANNOT BE SHARED. WHAT AM I?
LONELINESS.
SHOVE
THE RIDDLER
WEAPON OF CHOICE: RIDDLES
THE PENGUIN
WEAPON OF CHOICE: TRICK UMBRELLAS
WAAH!

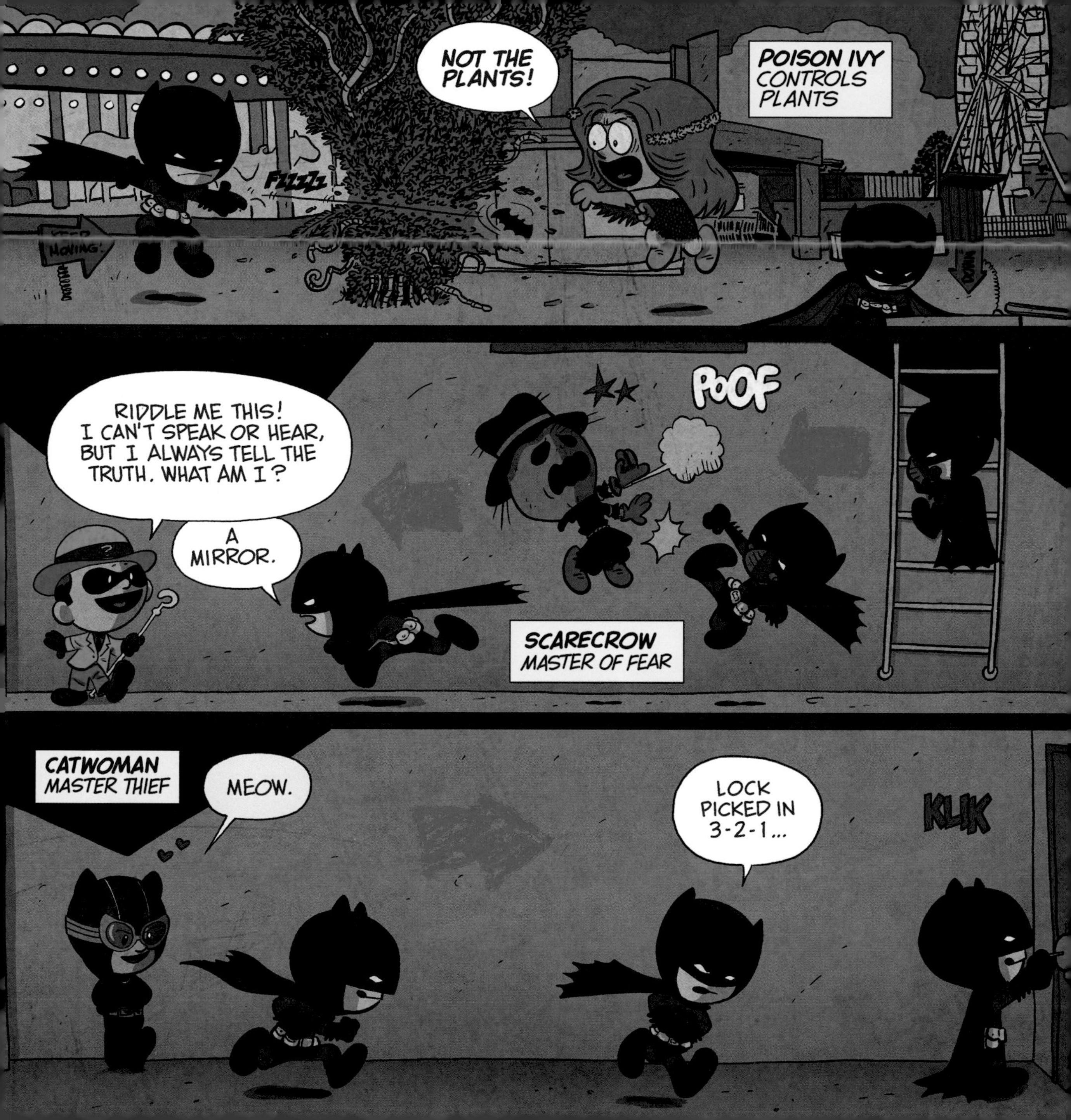
NOT THE PLANTS!
POISON IVY CONTROLS PLANTS
RIDDLE ME THIS! I CAN'T SPEAK OR HEAR, BUT I ALWAYS TELL THE TRUTH. WHAT AM I?
A MIRROR.
POOF
SCARECROW MASTER OF FEAR
CATWOMAN MASTER THIEF
MEOW.
LOCK PICKED IN 3-2-1...
KLIK

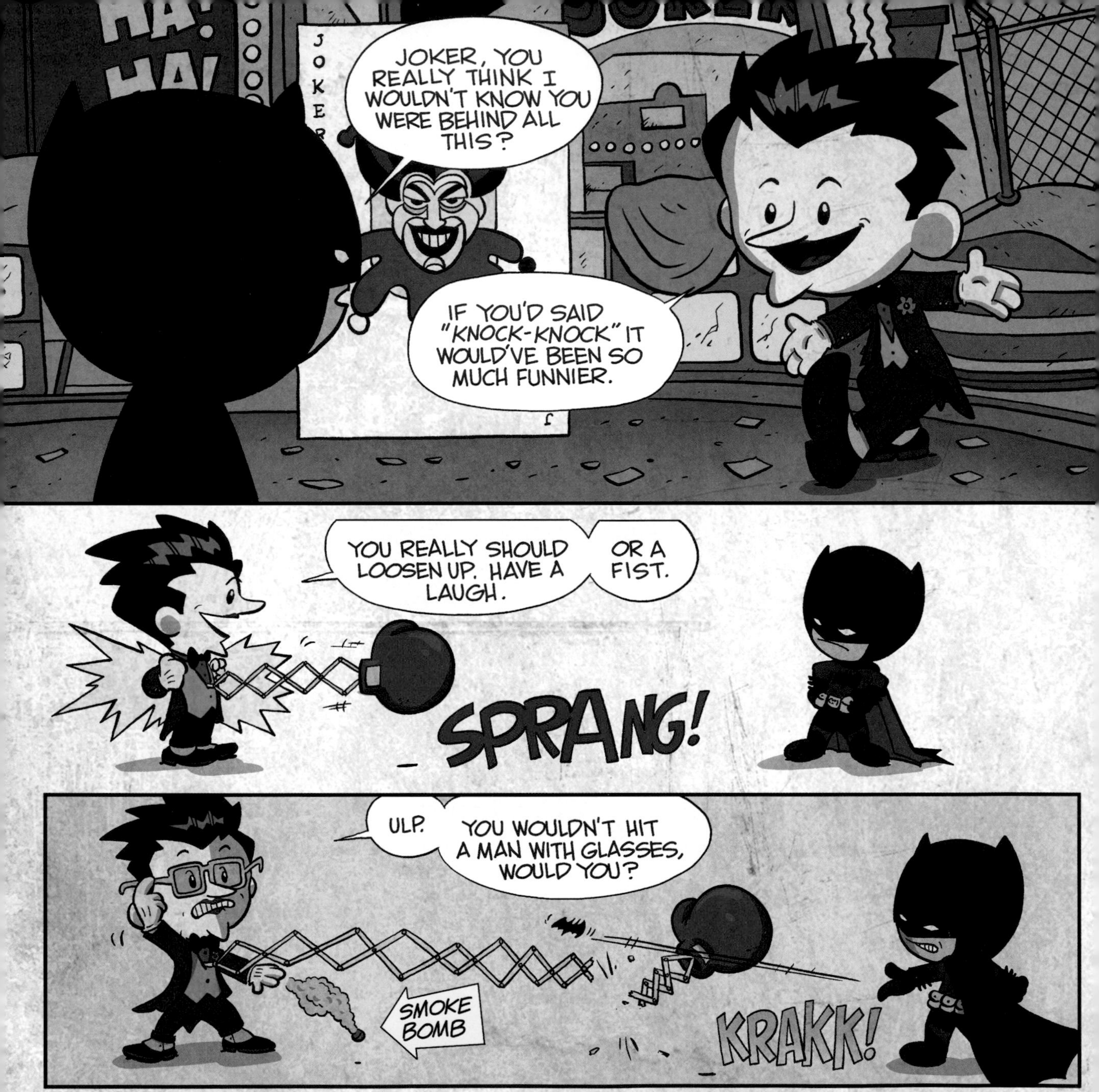
JOKER, YOU REALLY THINK I WOULDN'T KNOW YOU WERE BEHIND ALL THIS?
IF YOU'D SAID "KNOCK-KNOCK" IT WOULD'VE BEEN SO MUCH FUNNIER.
YOU REALLY SHOULD LOOSEN UP. HAVE A LAUGH.
OR A FIST.
SPRANG!
ULP.
YOU WOULDN'T HIT A MAN WITH GLASSES, WOULD YOU?
SMOKE BOMB
KRAKK!

People think fighting crime is an obsession—
something I have to do.

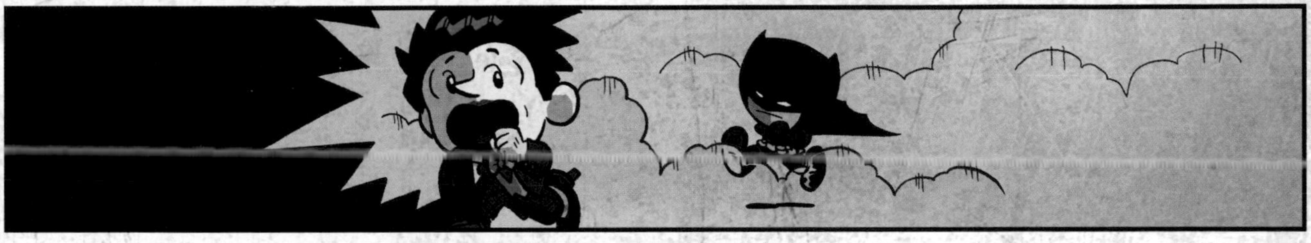

But I chose this life. I know what I'm doing.
And on any given day, I could stop doing it.

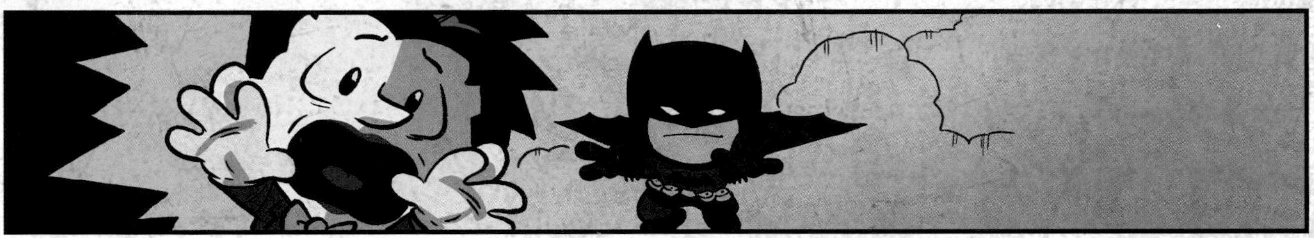

Today, however, isn't that day.
And tomorrow won't be either.

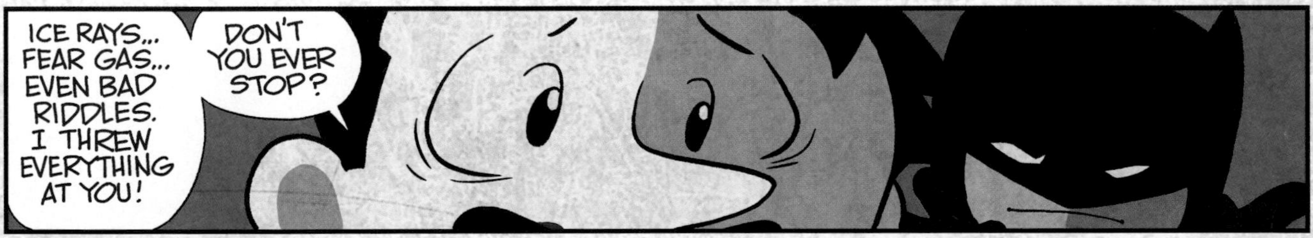
ICE RAYS... FEAR GAS... EVEN BAD RIDDLES. I THREW EVERYTHING AT YOU!
DON'T YOU EVER STOP?

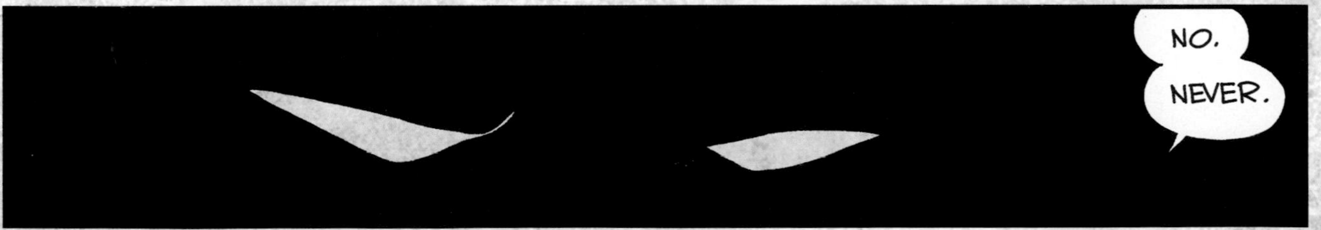
NO. NEVER.

In my life, I lost the people I loved most.
I didn't think I could recover. Yet here I am.
And I'll be here tomorrow,
and the night after that.
Someone tries to knock me to the ground every day.
"Stay down," they tell me.
And I tell them, "No. I will not."

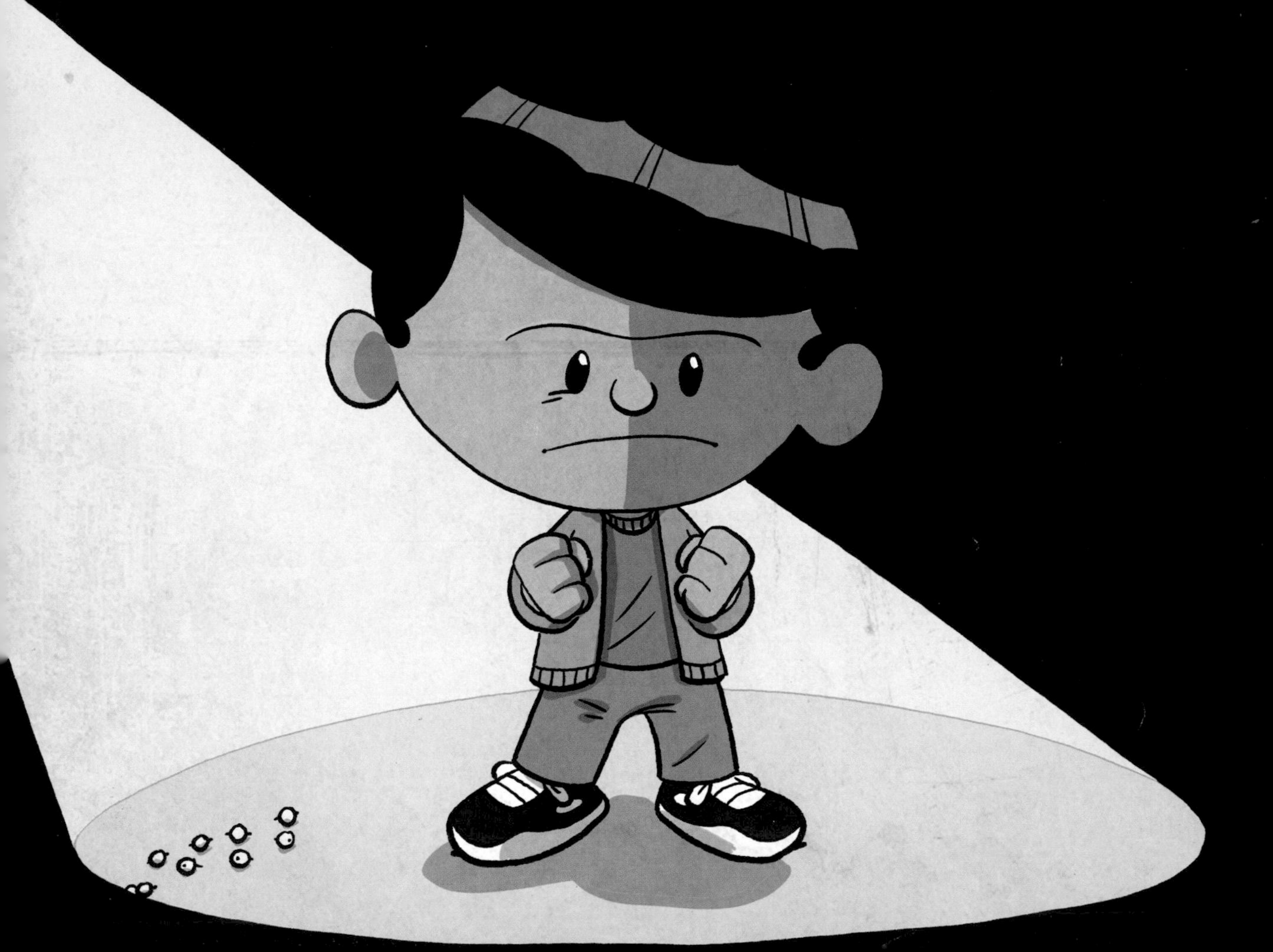

Everyone is scared sometimes.
We all feel pain—and we all have moments
when we get knocked down.
But why do we fall?
So we can learn to pick ourselves up.
There are times that will feel impossible,
but no matter how bad it gets, just remember...

You don't have to fight alone.

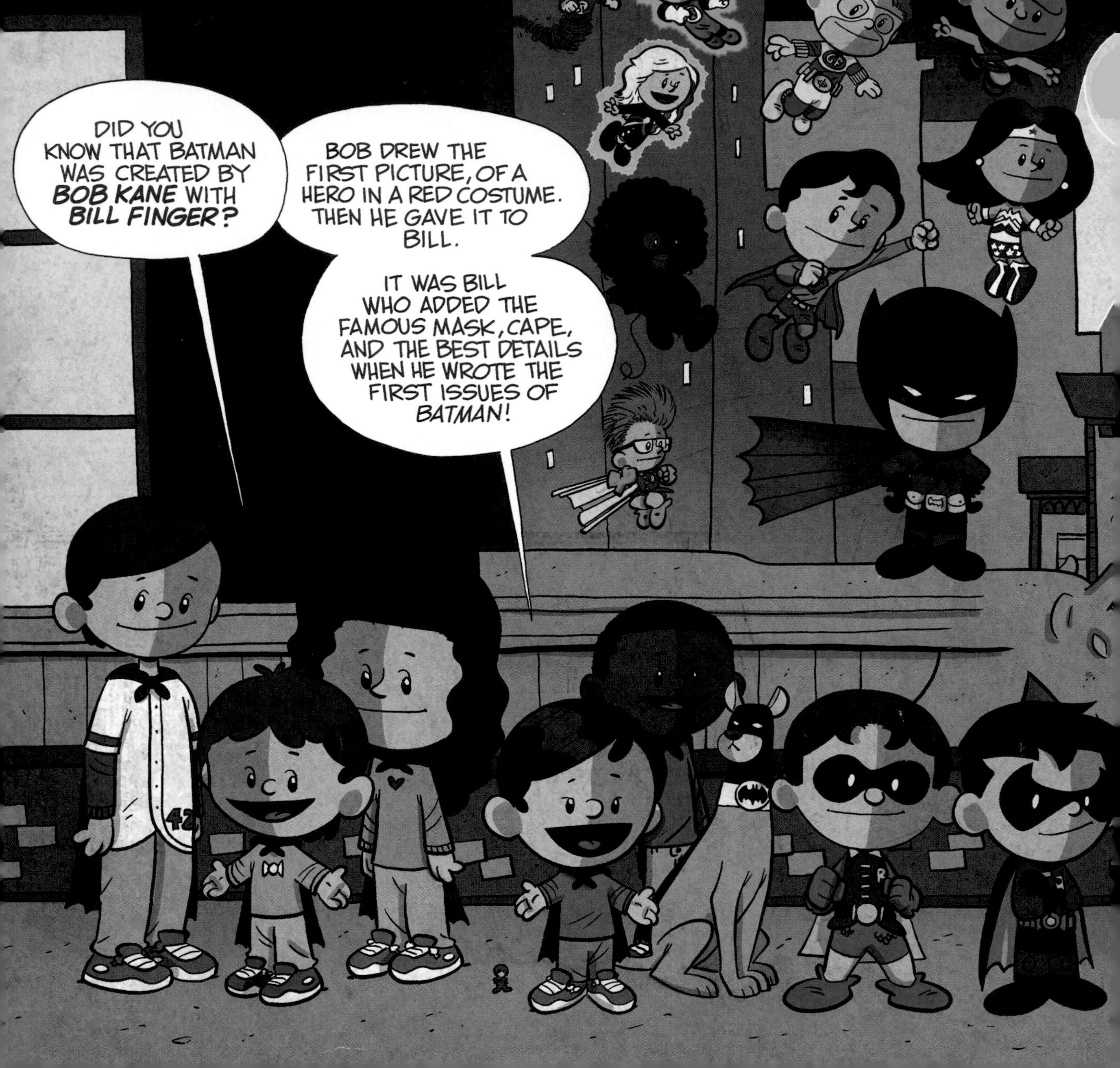
DID YOU KNOW THAT BATMAN WAS CREATED BY **BOB KANE** WITH **BILL FINGER**?
BOB DREW THE FIRST PICTURE, OF A HERO IN A RED COSTUME. THEN HE GAVE IT TO BILL.
IT WAS BILL WHO ADDED THE FAMOUS MASK, CAPE, AND THE BEST DETAILS WHEN HE WROTE THE FIRST ISSUES OF *BATMAN*!
42

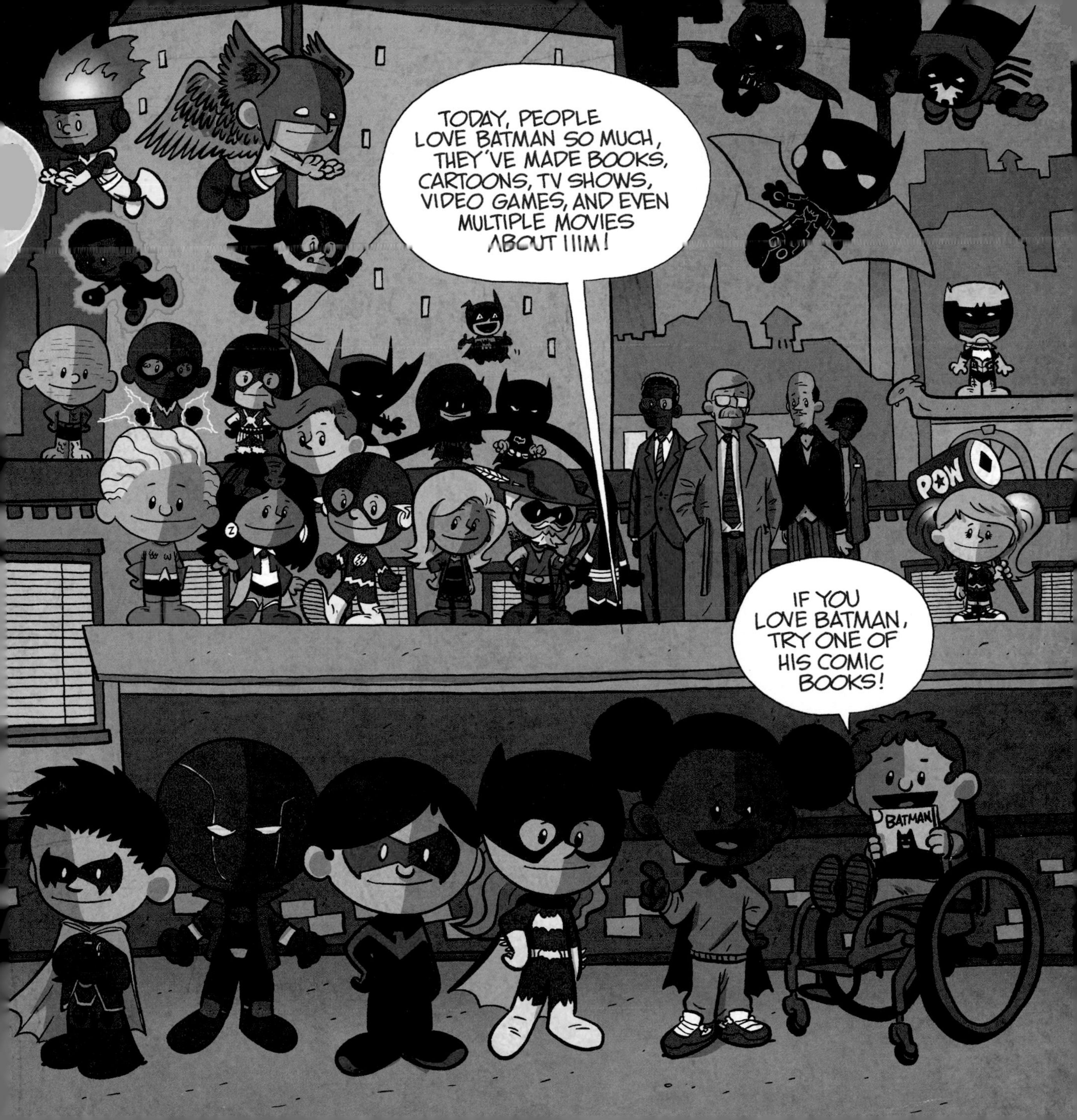
TODAY, PEOPLE LOVE BATMAN SO MUCH, THEY'VE MADE BOOKS, CARTOONS, TV SHOWS, VIDEO GAMES, AND EVEN MULTIPLE MOVIES ABOUT HIM!
IF YOU LOVE BATMAN, TRY ONE OF HIS COMIC BOOKS!
POW
BATMAN

They call me a Super Hero—
The Dark Knight, The World's Greatest Detective, The Caped Crusader—
but I don't have special powers.
I can't fly or lift a car over my head.
I'm an ordinary man, who will never, ever, ever give up.

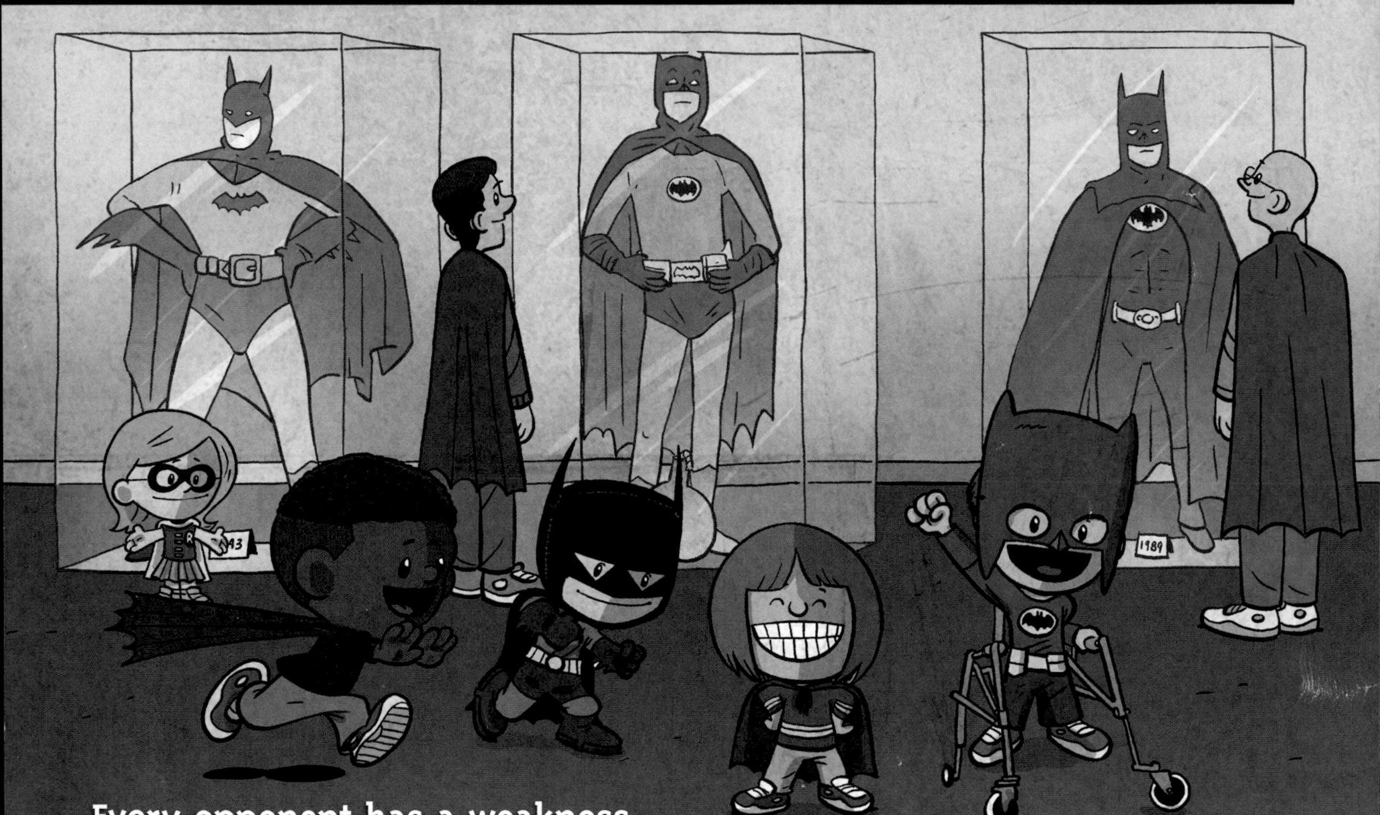
1989

Every opponent has a weakness.
Every problem has a solution.
Whatever challenge you face, your greatest weapon is your brain.
Your greatest power is your strength of character.
Study, prepare, outwork, and endure.

It's not the gadgets, the cars, or the money.

It's not the cave, the butler, or even the uniform.

Being Batman comes from what's underneath: the sheer will to face your fear... and the refusal to let them stop you.

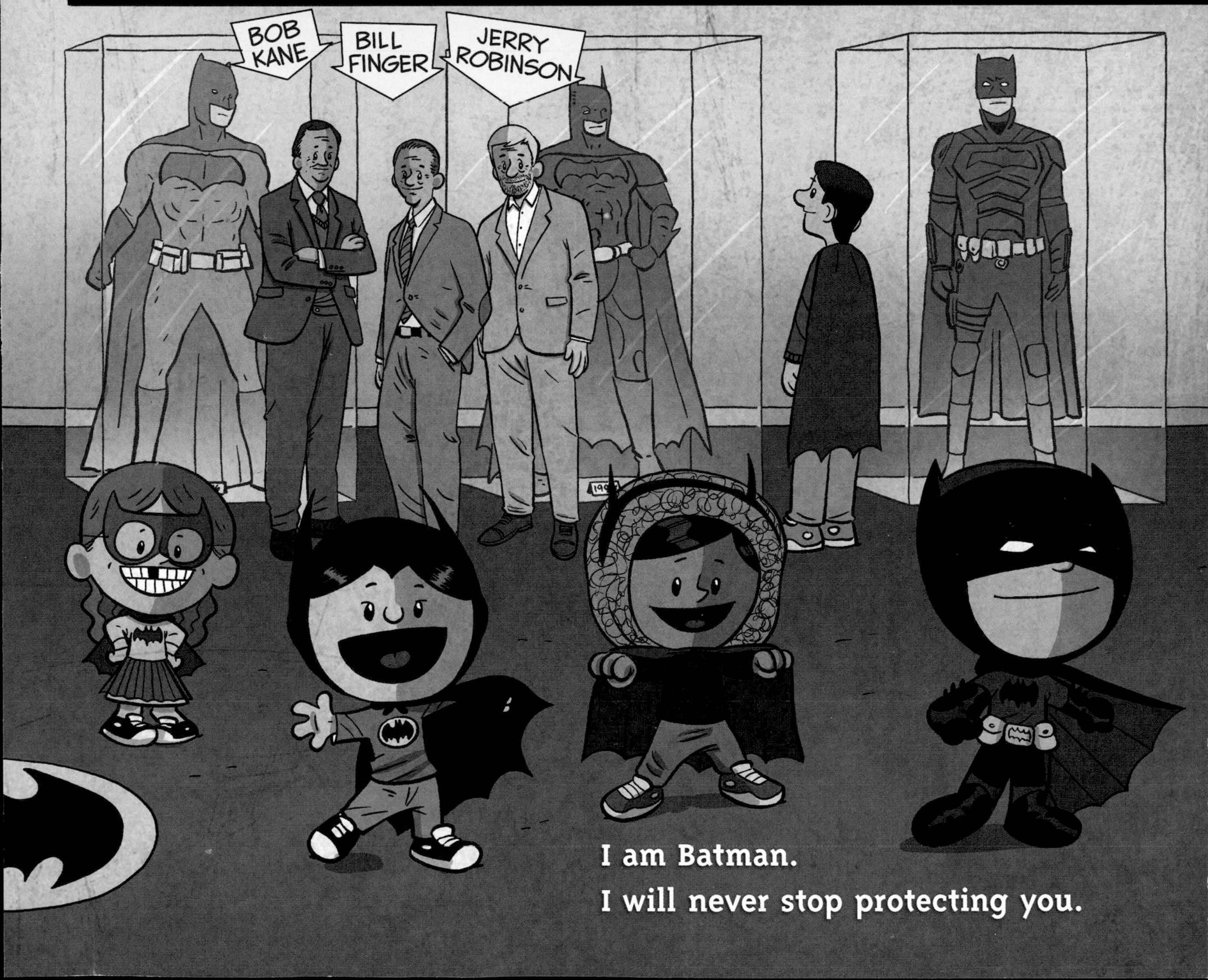
BOB KANE
BILL FINGER
JERRY ROBINSON

I am Batman.

I will never stop protecting you.

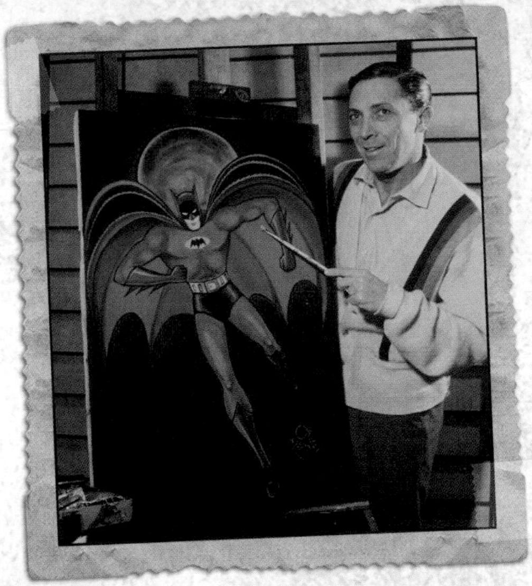

Bob Kane

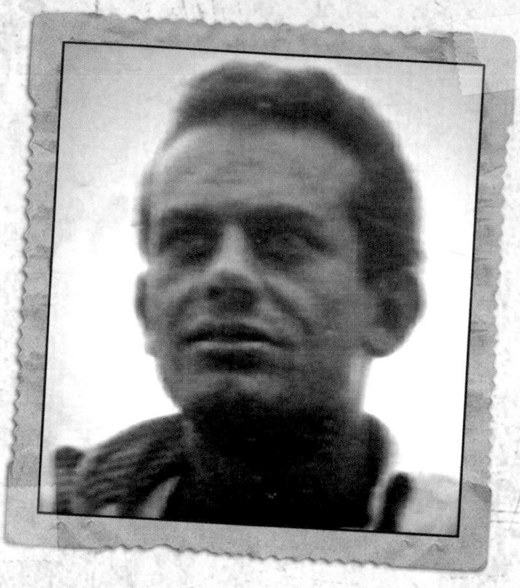

Bill Finger

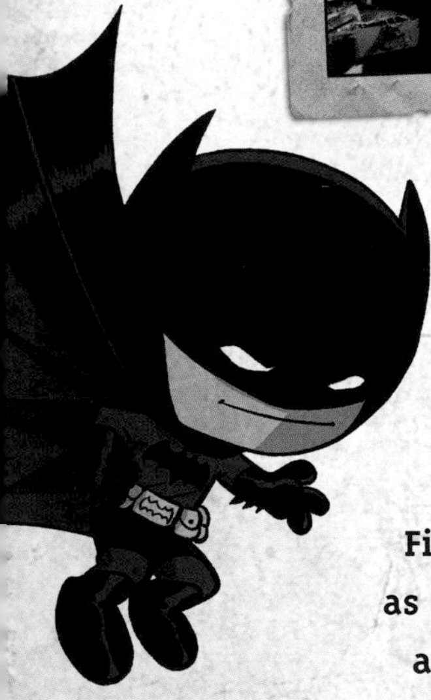

These are the creators of Batman:
artist **BOB KANE** and writer **BILL FINGER.**
In the late 1930s, Kane showed an initial drawing to Finger. Originally, the character had reddish tights and big bat wings.

Finger added the famous pointy-eared mask with white eyes as well as gloves, replaced the wings with a scalloped cape, and made the costume gray. Finger also added the name Bruce Wayne, Gotham City, and wrote the first issue as well as the origin of Batman.

Near the start of World War II, these two young Jewish men built a hero who was grounded in reality, with a level of depth and emotion that hadn't been seen before.

Their idea changed comic books—and showed the world the power of an ordinary person.

Timeline

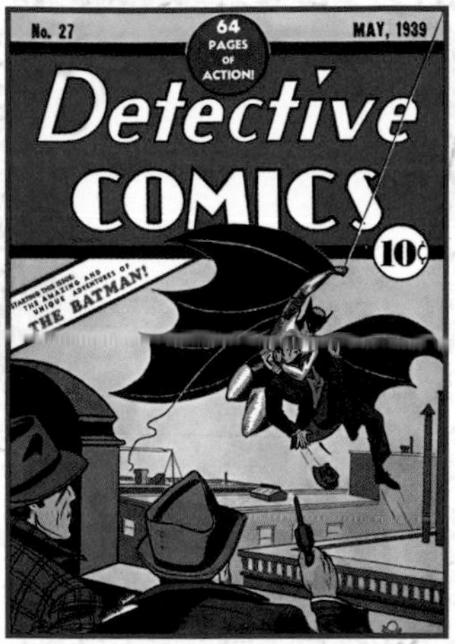
No. 27
64 PAGES OF ACTION!
MAY, 1939
Detective COMICS
10¢

1939

Detective Comics #27
by Bob Kane and Bill Finger

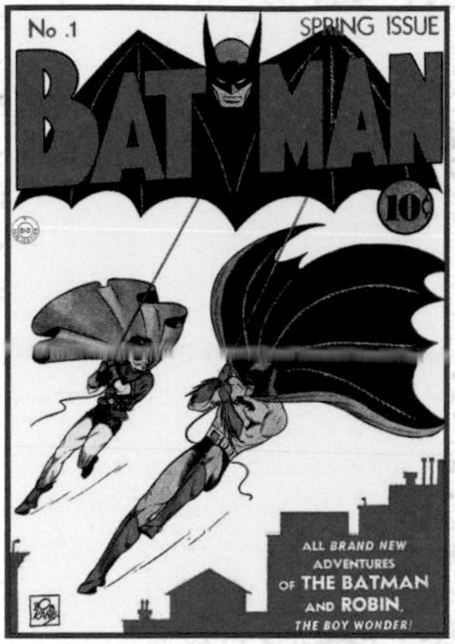
No. 1
SPRING ISSUE
BATMAN
10¢
ALL BRAND NEW ADVENTURES OF THE BATMAN AND ROBIN, THE BOY WONDER!

1940

Batman #1
by Bob Kane, Bill Finger, and Jerry Robinson

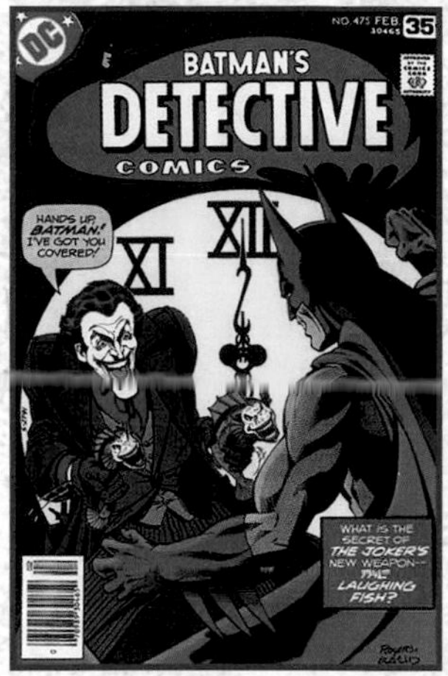
NO. 475 FEB.
35
BATMAN'S
DETECTIVE
COMICS
HANDS UP, BATMAN! I'VE GOT YOU COVERED!
XI
XII
WHAT IS THE SECRET OF THE JOKER'S NEW WEAPON-- THE LAUGHING FISH?

1978

Detective Comics #475
by Steve Englehart, Marshall Rogers, and Terry Austin
(the first comic Brad Meltzer ever owned)

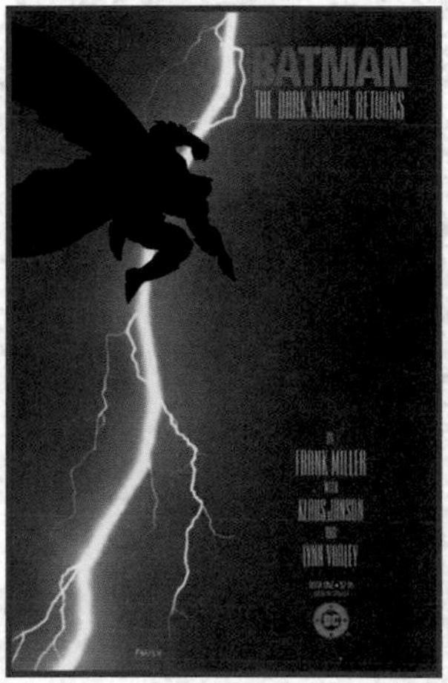
BATMAN
THE DARK KNIGHT RETURNS
BY FRANK MILLER WITH KLAUS JANSON AND LYNN VARLEY

1986

Batman: The Dark Knight Returns #1
by Frank Miller, Klaus Janson, and Lynn Varley

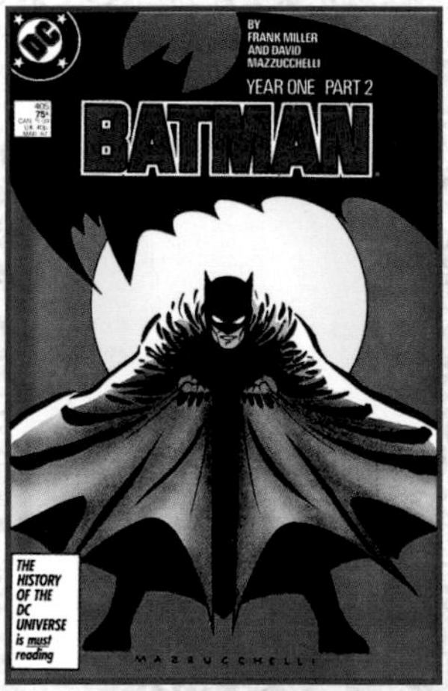
BY FRANK MILLER AND DAVID MAZZUCCHELLI
YEAR ONE PART 2
BATMAN
THE HISTORY OF THE DC UNIVERSE is must reading
MAZZUCCHELLI

1987

Batman #405
by Frank Miller and David Mazzucchelli

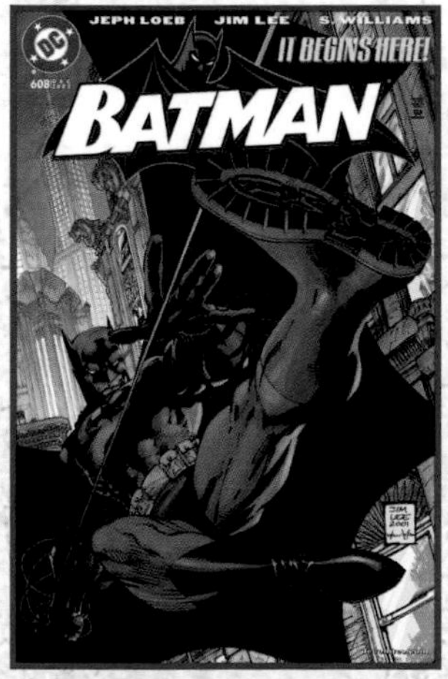
JEPH LOEB
JIM LEE
S. WILLIAMS
IT BEGINS HERE!
BATMAN

2002

Batman #608
by Jeph Loeb, Jim Lee, Scott Williams, and Alex Sinclair

For Jonas,
who understands the true power of determination

And in memory of my grandfather Ben Rubin,
for telling me my favorite Batman story
—B.M.

For Jason Kaplan,
a comic book fan,
a Batman fan,
a good guy
—C.E.

To show you the very best that Batman has to offer, we used scenes from actual Batman stories whenever possible. For more incredible Batman tales, we recommend and acknowledge the below works. We also wouldn't be here without Bill Finger, Bob Kane, Jerry Robinson, and the thousands of other creators who make Batman who he is.

Special thanks to Jim Lee, Marie Javins, and all our family at DC and Warner Bros., including Melanie Swartz and Benjamin Harper, and to superfriends Geoff Johns, Noah Kuttler, Nick Marell, Michael Green, and Marc Tyler Nobleman for their input of early drafts, as well as Paul Levitz, Dan DiDio, Frank Miller, David Mazzucchelli, Alan Moore, Brian Bolland, Jeph Loeb, Grant Morrison, Chip Kidd, Gary Frank, Tom King, Steve Englehart, Marshall Rogers, Neal Adams, Marv Wolfman, Adam West, Burt Ward, Tim Burton, Christopher Nolan, Judd Winick, and especially Bob Schreck for first inviting Brad to the Hall of Justice. Extra love to Teri and Stu Meltzer for letting Brad dress as Batman every year for Halloween.

SOURCES

Detective Comics #27 by Bill Finger and Bob Kane
The Dark Knight Returns by Frank Miller
Batman: Year One by Frank Miller and David Mazzucchelli
Detective Comics #168 by Bill Finger, Lew Sayre Schwartz, and Win Mortimer
Detective Comics #475 by Steve Englehart and Marshall Rogers
Batman: Hush by Jeph Loeb and Jim Lee
The Killing Joke by Alan Moore and Brian Bolland
Batman #681—Batman RIP by Grant Morrison and Tony Daniel
Batman #20—I am Bane by Tom King and David Finch
JLA: New World Order by Grant Morrison and Howard Porter
Identity Crisis by Brad Meltzer and Rags Morales
Under the Hood by Judd Winick, Doug Mahnke, Eric Battle, and Shane Davis
Batman: Earth One by Geoff Johns and Gary Frank
Batman (1966 TV show)
Batman (1989 film)—directed by Tim Burton
Batman Begins—directed by Christopher Nolan
Gotham (2014 TV show)
Superman/Batman: Apocalypse—the Animated Movie
Batman: The Animated Series
Bill the Boy Wonder: The Secret Co-Creator of Batman by Marc Tyler Nobleman

DIAL BOOKS FOR YOUNG READERS
An imprint of Penguin Random House LLC, New York

First published in the United States of America by Dial Books for Young Readers, an imprint of Penguin Random House LLC, 2022

Batman created by Bob Kane with Bill Finger

Stories Change the World is a trademark of Forty-four Steps, Inc. • Coloring by K.J. Díaz with Christopher Eliopoulos

Dial and colophon are registered trademarks of Penguin Random House LLC. • Visit us online at penguinrandomhouse.com.

Library of Congress Cataloging-in-Publication Data is available. • Photo of Bob Kane: ABC Photo Archives/Disney General Entertainment Content via Getty Images. Photo of Bill Finger courtesy of Athena Finger.

ISBN 9780593531464 • Printed in the USA • 10 9 8 7 6 5 4 3 2 1
PC • Designed by Jason Henry • Text set in Triplex • The artwork for this book was created digitally.

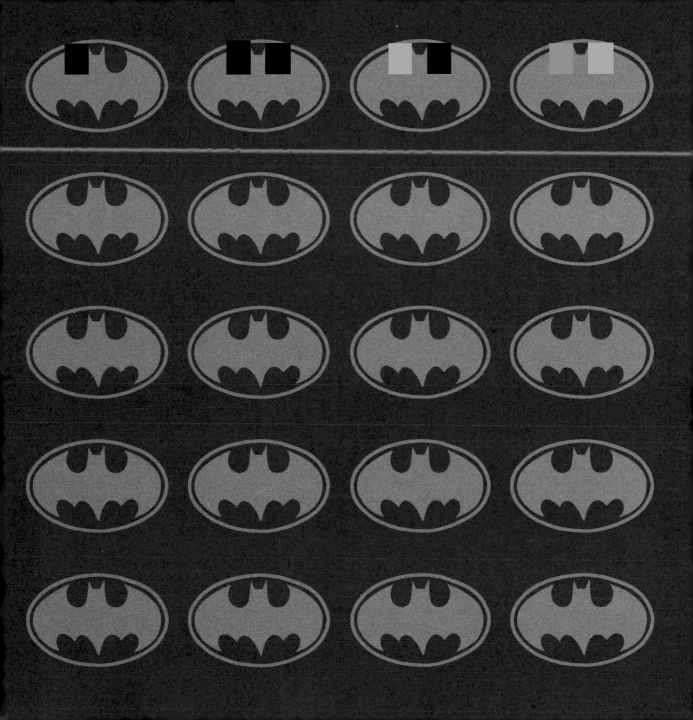

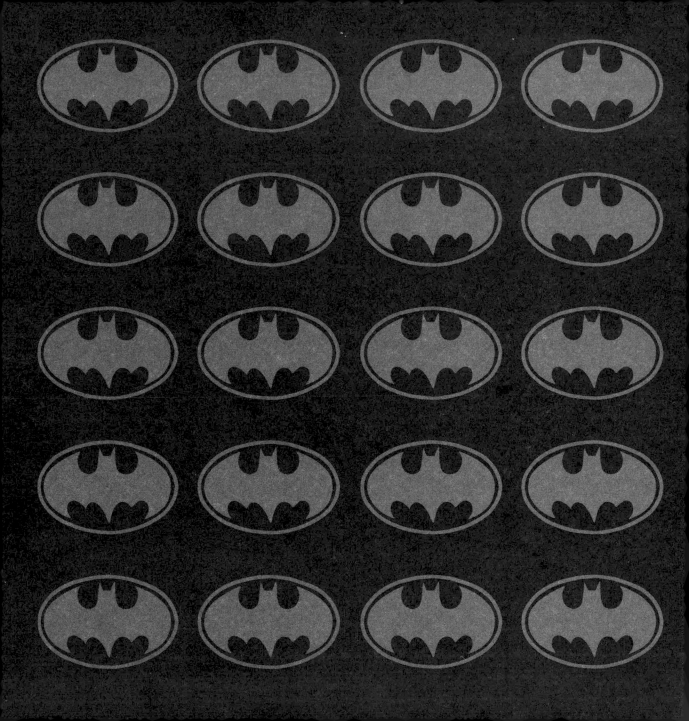